I WAS THERE THE NIGHT HE DIED

I Was There the Night He Died

Ray Robertson

BIBLIOASIS

WINDSOR, ONTARIO

3 1969 02249 9171

FIRST EDITION

Library and Archives Canada Cataloguing in Publication

Robertson, Ray, 1966-, author
    I was there the night he died / written by Ray Robertson.

Issued in print and electronic formats.
ISBN 978-1-927428-69-6 (pbk.).--ISBN 978-1-927428-70-2 (epub)

I. Title.

PS8585.O3219I2 2014   C813'.54   C2013-907285-3
                                                      C2013-907286-1

Edited by Dan Wells
Copy-edited by Zachariah Wells
Typeset by Chris Andrechek
Cover designed by Bill Douglas

 Canada Council Conseil des Arts
for the Arts du Canada

  ONTARIO ARTS COUNCIL
CONSEIL DES ARTS DE L'ONTARIO
50 YEARS OF ONTARIO GOVERNMENT SUPPORT OF THE ARTS
50 ANS DE SOUTIEN DU GOUVERNEMENT DE L'ONTARIO AUX ARTS

Canadian Patrimoine
Heritage canadien

Biblioasis acknowledges the ongoing financial support of the Government of Canada through the Canada Council for the Arts, Canadian Heritage, the Canada Book Fund; and the Government of Ontario through the Ontario Arts Council.

The author acknowledges the support of the Ontario Arts Council and the Toronto Arts Council.

PRINTED AND BOUND IN CANADA

 MIX
Paper from
responsible sources
FSC
www.fsc.org FSC® C107923

Mara Korkola
Again, of course

Dan Wells
C-town boy with an A-1 ear

Everything is not enough
Nothing is too much to bear
—Townes Van Zandt

CHAPTER ONE

WHAT THE HELL, WHY NOT tell the truth?

Within reason of course. Too much of anything, it seems, is never a good idea.

"Sorry," the teenager sitting next to me says, needing to get by me to go to the restroom for the third time since we left Toronto.

"Sure," I say, standing up, letting him slide past. Since we pulled out of Union Station less than two hours ago he's watched half of a T & A-spiked action movie on his laptop, slayed forty-five minutes worth of black-hooded cartoon terrorists on the same, and made and received enough phone calls and text messages that there's absolutely nothing going on out there he doesn't know about. And washed down a large bag of Doritos with a can of Red Bull and another of Diet Coke.

When Sara and I used to visit my parents—Sara driving, me in charge of changing the CDs and keeping Barney, our overweight Black Lab, from climbing into the front seat when the steaming bag of Harvey's takeout we'd always pick up on the way out of town was finally unwrapped—by the time we'd get to Chatham I'd be ankle-deep in vegetarian burger wrappers and empty french-fry cartons and soft-drink containers and crushed Tim Horton's cups and a medium-size Timbits box, only a few dough-and-lard survivors left rolling around inside.

I pull open the sports section, the only part of the newspaper I ever bother with, and concentrate on the scoring summaries from last night's games. *Kronwall 4 (Datsyuk, Zetterberg), 13:36* makes a lot more sense than thinking about Sara. Or Barney or my mother or even my father, the only one of them still alive, if only in body, Alzheimer's almost done with its first cruel course—his mind—and in no particular hurry, it seems, to devour what's left.

I fold the newspaper in two and slide it underneath my seat and pull the notepad and pen from my shirt pocket. Even a dominating Red Wings road win can't distract death thoughts; only doing—doing and doing, *nada*-negating doing—doing the trick. And it *is* a trick. There's a hole and you fill it and as soon as you stop shoveling, it's empty again. Not including the rapid inhalation of an eight ball of good cocaine, however, it's the only magic I know, so I do what I do, scribble and revise and scribble some more until I notice that the boy is standing in the aisle beside my seat. I have no idea how long he's been waiting there. Now it's my turn to say I'm sorry.

Sitting back down and sticking in his earbuds for another go round with all those pesky terrorists, "You looked busy," he says.

That's the plan, I almost say, before realizing that that's exactly the sort of thing someone in a novel might say.

"Yeah" is what I do say, but it's too late, the kid's already got both earbuds in, his fingers are already busy at his keypad.

*   *   *

LET'S GET THIS STRAIGHT. I'M NOT IN DENIAL. Nothing has been repressed. I haven't bypassed my pain. And what I'm most not is haunted. Only people in sentimental movies and overwritten novels are haunted. I'm sad. Real fucking sad.

If anything, my grief has been too perfect—textbook, practically.

I said goodbye to Sara seventeen months ago at a quarter to nine on a Tuesday morning, the same thing I did every Monday through Friday when she left for work at the OSPCA, and by 4:30 PM I was making funeral arrangements. Three days later Sara was in the ground and the world went back to work and Sara was my dead wife, Sara. That's called Stage One: Numbness or Shock.

I felt a tightness in my throat. I always seemed to be short of breath. All I wanted to do was sleep. I sighed all the time. The police said the accident might have been her fault, she possibly merged when she shouldn't have, and when I wasn't too tired, I was angry at her for that in particular and for dying in general. I was also furious at myself because my last words to her had been a reminder to please not forget to pick up vodka when she went wine shopping on the way home from work. That's known as Stage Two: Disorganization.

Days and then weeks and then months and then the lie that everyone tells you actually becomes true: minutes, hours even, when you think about something other than your grief. I knew I was beginning to get better when, ten months or so after Sara's death, I was putting my change in the dish on top of the refrigerator and a quarter fell to the floor and rolled underneath the fridge and I took out my notebook from the middle drawer of my desk for the first time since the accident and wondered why it was that any time anything gets dropped on the kitchen floor it invariably ends up underneath the fridge, a minor mystery to be pondered right along with where the hell all the missing single socks go and why it is that obese people always own tiny dogs. That's referred to as Stage Three: Re-organization.

There isn't any Stage Four.

* * *

THE OLD TOWN LOOKS THE SAME as I step down from the train; except that J.P.'s, the strip club next door to the Via station that for decades has been keeping it shaking, has burned down, and another Goodwill has sprouted up down the street since the last time I was here just a month ago, arson and charity clothing stores Chatham's two biggest growth industries. Uncle Donny is waiting for me inside his idling Buick.

"What do you know for sure, pal?"

"Not much," I say, putting my bags in the back seat.

"Well, that makes two of us."

It's the same exchange we've been having since I was six years old and I've got no reason to doubt he's telling me the truth. I once based a character in one of my novels on Uncle Donny. The nice thing about being a writer from Southwestern Ontario is that the people you tend to write about don't mind your utilizing their likenesses. Of course, on the down side, they don't mind because they don't care, voluntary reading as dubious an adult occupation as, say, Chinese shadow puppet theatre or antique rug collecting.

"How is he?" I say.

"Good. Fine. He'll be glad to see you."

We both know that's a lie, but I don't mind hearing it if he's willing to say it.

"Goddamnit, goddamn Phaneuf, sonofabitch could go into the goddamn corner with an egg in his pocket and come out with it unbroken." Uncle Donny thumps the dash with an open palm, punishment for the radio broadcasting the bad news of another Maple Leaf goal against, this time the direct result of a Dion Phaneuf giveaway. Uncle Donny is as much a Leaf fan as Dad and I are Red Wings supporters, but his anger seems a little disproportionate for just another nail in the coffin of just another Toronto loss. Four decades and counting of Stanley Cup futility have a way of taking the edge off one's competitive intensity. Besides, no matter who's playing on the radio, Rat Pack casino concert tapes (and, now, CDs) have always been Uncle Donny's car sounds of choice, Frank and Dean and Sammy's corny jokes and schmaltzy songs as much a somatic reminder of riding with Uncle Donny as the perennial pine tree air freshener dangling from the rearview mirror. He catches me staring at him muttering into the pop can at his lips.

"You want to stop by the house?" he says. "So you can drop off your things?"

"Let's go there first."

Uncle Donny clicks on the turn signal. "You're the boss."

There is Thames View Gardens, a nursing home that has a self-contained Alzheimer's ward. Just as hometown aesthetic indifference has its professional advantages, I should be thankful that as Chatham's population has actually decreased since I left for university twenty-five years ago, senior citizens' homes and extended care units have proportionally increased. Dad was on a waiting list for less than forty-eight hours before they found him his spot at Thames View. Chatham, Ontario: out with the young, stuck with the old.

It's only just after seven PM when we pull into the parking lot, but it's already dark—late-January sleety too—none of which stops Uncle Donny from waving me inside so he can have a cigarette outside the automatic front doors. The few thin strands of black hair he insists on still greasing and combing straight back do what they're told in spite of the wind.

"When your Grandmother was at St. Andrew's I used to smoke right in her room," he says. "You'd think that the person living there paying the bills would be the one to make that decision, if you ask me."

I don't ask him—just tell him I'll see him inside—and leave him to his Player's Light. He could have smoked on the way over, but he's here almost every day, meaning I haven't had to be, so I let him have his five minutes of cloudy quiet. Aside from me, Uncle Donny is Dad's only living relative, five other brothers and sisters Chatham-born and Chatham-buried, most from cancer. No one's bragging about it, but Chatham is Canada's cancer capital. Instead of the sign on Highway Six that announces

WELCOME TO CHATHAM, ONTARIO:
HOME OF BASEBALL HALL OF FAMER FERGUSON JENKINS

maybe the Chamber of Commerce should change it to:

CHATHAM, ONTARIO:
ALL THE PROBLEMS OF A BIG CITY WITH ALL
THE INCONVENIENCES OF A SMALL TOWN

We only moved Dad into Thames View Gardens last summer, but I'd been inside the building itself plenty of times before, most unmemorably May 15 forty-four years ago, when I was born here, when instead of exclusively seeing lives out, Thames View Gardens was St. Joseph's Hospital and routinely saw them in. My parents wanted children, couldn't have children, then, when they were both in their mid-thirties and resigned to being childless, discovered they were going to have a child—me.

You have to walk past general reception to get to the Alzheimer's ward, as well as the empty dining room, the locked exercise room, and the recreation room where, behind a closed door, someone at a piano is competing to be heard over a chorus of cracked voices singing "Camptown Races." As hard as it is to get used to your father being a mute, expressionless, staring stranger, imagining him joining in on an after-dinner senior-citizen sing-a-long is even more difficult. Even novelists have their limits.

Dad and his three roommates (fellow residents? patients?) have been fed and cleaned up and are pillow-propped-up in bed and settling in for their evening's indifference to anything but the six inches or so directly in front of their faces. Thames View is the best Alzheimer's care facility in town, but even when, as now, the gag-inducing smell of fresh human feces has been assiduously scrubbed away, the nostril-hair-tingling tang of powerful disinfectants reminds you of what it's hiding. There are family members gathered at two of the other beds, but since no one here knows me, there are only stoical nods from the men and sad, knowing smiles from the women, the children—or grandchildren, more accurately—probably at the vending machines in the basement if they've been coaxed into coming at all. I give Dad a hug that he endures like an unexpected but painless back spasm and sit down on the chair beside the bed.

If Uncle Donny was here we could shoot the breeze and I wouldn't feel as if I was ignoring Dad, that Dad, as usual, was just letting his older brother blather, happy to not get too involved. Everyone knows the rudiments of the Alzheimer's patient's shutdown countdown, a little less of the loved one a little more each day until there's no missing person's report that'll ever bring them back, but this suffocating silence still feels odd and I don't know what to do other than what I'm doing, resting my hand on Dad's forearm. Until I realize it looks like I'm pinning his arm to the bed, so I don't even do that.

I stand up and Dad doesn't notice, doesn't even blink, eyes open but dull. I'm going to be back tomorrow, and the day after that, and the day after that, so I excuse myself for leaving early, lean over and give him a hug goodbye.

Brut.

Somebody has remembered to dab some of his favourite cologne on him. My mother used to buy it for him at Shopper's Drug Mart. $3.99 bought you a year's worth of smelling like what a man smelt like. My dad, he was a *Brut* man.

I kiss him goodbye on his cheek, something I've never done before, and breathe in deep the cheap cologne, and there you go, there you are, a K-Mart Blue Light Proustian Special, one stiff sniff and right back where you started, his guiding hand on your very first bike ride and a skinned right knee but that's all right, and how cool would it be if it pours tonight because the sound of the rain beating on the roof of the tent pitched in your parents' backyard is, like, so incredibly, totally awesome.

Everything that matters already happened. Everything since then is just the same thing but different. The decades and decades since your first Pixy Stix and purple Kool-Aid high and your last strictly-against-doctor's-orders rye and ginger ale only seem like several persons ago, are only the nice fib we tell ourselves about how everybody—everybody including you, too, of course—grows up.

Look: when Jerry Garcia died of a heart attack while detoxing from years of heroin abuse at some California get-well nightmare called Serenity Knolls, they found him curled up in bed in the fetal position cuddling an apple and with a fat smile on his face. The guy was 53 years old. Sure he was.

* * *

AND THAT'S AN ACTUAL FACT, that's the truth, that's exactly the sort of thing I'm talking about. *Lives of the Poets (with Guitars)* is what I'm calling it. Picking up where Dr. Johnson left off 250 years ago, I'll add ample electricity and put a good goosing to the good doctor's definition of our shared subject so as to include more than what's merely written down vertically rather than horizontally, real poetry really being about greater rather than lesser heat. And what could be hotter than the buzz saw assault of Johnny Ramone's Mosrite Venture guitar or Howlin' Wolf's larynx-shredding voice or Gene Clark's grievy minor key mood pieces? And just because any book composed of one hundred percent facts is as limiting as one woven entirely out of lies, I'll include a little make-believe dollop on top, each chapter beginning with the same elegiac incantation, "I was there the night he died," the lament of my surprisingly erudite and well-travelled sixty-something ex-roadie narrator who's uniquely qualified to comment upon not only the lives but the deaths of my real-life musical subjects. I've even got an epigraph ready, a compositional compass to help keep me on track, from Ford Maddox Ford's *The March of Literature*: "For it is your hot love for your art, not your dry delvings in the dry bones of ana and philologies that will enable you to convey to others your strong passion." *Hot love.* I mean, really, how can you go wrong with that?

Because what I'm not going to do is write a novel about Sara dying. And not because it's too painful to consider or too difficult to do or because it's wrong to wring ink and paper gladness from flesh and blood sadness. Novelists are nervous vampires who depend upon the busily living for their sedentary livelihood, and Sara was always a very willing victim. Our lust, our lies, our love: all of it is in there in one fictionalized form or another in one or another book, Sara only really objecting once, when, out of laziness or puckishness, I can't remember which, I'd called the character based on her *Sarah*.

But you don't even spell your name that way. Anyone who knows us will understand that it's not you.

This is what is called looking the victim horse in the mouth. As in vampires should be content to make it alive and still sucking in the morning. As in vampires should learn not to push their luck. I changed the character's name to *Mary*.

I'm not going to write a novel about Sara dying because writing a novel makes things go away. A novel is one long delicious scratch that makes the itching stop for good. A novel is a two-year puke of pain and pleasure that cleans out the sweet poison inside entirely, at last.

But if you lose the poison, you lose its root cause, too. I don't want to lose my roots. My roots are mine.

* * *

DROPPING ME OFF FROM Thames View Gardens, Uncle Donny doesn't offer to come inside to help get me settled or to wait idling in the driveway to make sure my key works, doesn't even give me a good luck wave goodbye. He does what he's always done, races into the street in reverse without bothering to look behind him and honks, once, when he's almost out of sight. I hear it after I've set my bags down and am closing the front door.

Not that there's much reason to bother bolting the door—locking up is a Toronto tick, where there aren't subdivisions named Buttercup Village and people occasionally wander further than their front doors on the way to their cars—but I do it anyway and let the streetlight out front light my way through the living room and into the kitchen where I know there's a switch. My parents moved here five years ago, just before my mother died of a stroke, just before the first discernible signs of Alzheimer's afflicted my father, and I'm still not used to the layout of their would-be dream house: large, unlandscaped front and back lawns for him to work and worry over, two floors of brand new appliances and shiny fixtures and wall-to-wall spongy fresh carpeting for her to happily wear herself out cleaning. At least she died in action, the vacuum cleaner still humming when Dad found her collapsed on the bedroom floor. He hadn't been so lucky, had only gotten as far as laying down the sod before he began peeing off the front step and not remembering why he'd brought his shovel with him into the bathroom.

The lights work, but the taps are dead and the heat vents too, so I go down to the basement to check the furnace. It's not the pilot light—there is no pilot light—the furnace almost as cold to the touch as the inside of the freezer still three-quarters full of rump roasts and snow-entombed bags of peas and corn. Uncle Donny has been looking after Dad's bills for a while now, but apparently the water and gas bills haven't been on his to-do list lately. Ignoring Dad's power tools, Mum's collection of orthopedic shoes, and the boxed and electrical tape-sealed plastic Christmas tree that's seen its last Buttercup Village Christmas, I go back upstairs where at least it's only cold, not damp and cold. One of the reasons I'm here is to decide what to do with a lifetime's worth of valuables that aren't valuable anymore, but difficult decisions are what tomorrows are made for.

I never noticed before how many framed photographs my parents had of me. Of Sara and me. After Barney died not long after Sara, the discovery of an old tennis ball long-forgotten underneath the couch could instantly wound. Of course I knew he was gone; it was the sudden stab of remembering that he'd lived that ached. I did my best to make sure that every errant ball, every half-chewed bone, every well-gummed, stolen sock of mine was collected and boxed and waiting for the new dog I keep telling myself I'm going to get one day. I walk from room to room turning pictures of Sara and me face down.

I sit on the couch without taking off my coat and pick up the remote. Without the cable being connected, though, there's no picture, not even angry fuzz, nor even—like when I was a kid and we got our signal from the antenna on the roof—mute ghost people hidden behind the silencing snowstorm filling up the screen. I click off the TV. I should probably smoke a joint. This is probably a perfect example of one of those times when I should smoke a joint.

Marijuana has never made much sense to me, no more than non-alcoholic beer. Just like why someone would want to get fat without getting drunk, if you're going to get high, why choose a drug that makes you lazier, dozier, even more slow-witted than you already are? Unless, perhaps, you have a debilitating psychological predilection for jumpy drugs in general and dextroamphetamine sulfate in particular; in that case, pass the doobie, brother, and let that soothing smoke do its dumbing-down job. It was either that or take up yoga. I bought my first quarter ounce of weed just before I left Toronto.

I stand over the kitchen sink and light the joint and inhale and hold it in as best I can, but still cough a non-smoker's cough until my eyes begin to water. I push the ash that's accumulated in the hacking interim down the drain. Even if I can manage to get this shit in my lungs, I can't do it in here, my Mother at any moment about to float into the kitchen with a ghost dustpan and broom. Besides, it can't be much colder outside. Uncle Donny neglecting to pay the water bill at least ensured that the pipes didn't freeze. He must have drained them at some point too, which shows uncharacteristic foresight, like he knew that the water was going to be cut off.

Because my parents were among the first to buy a lot in the new subdivision, they were lucky enough to get what is perhaps Buttercup Village's premier location, a corner lot right next to the postage-stamp-sized park that separates their house from their nearest neighbor. I sit down on the single bench which is located directly underneath the single tree which stands right beside the small sign that tells you where you are and what you should be doing.

BUTTERCUP VILLAGE PARKETTTE
ENJOY!

I stick the joint between my lips and cup my mouth with one hand, pull the lighter out of my coat pocket with my other. I'm only worried about the wind, not nosey neighbors, people willingly on foot in the daytime in Chatham an anomaly, after eleven o'clock at night down-right abnormal. Just to be sure, I look left and then right and see all there is to see, identical darkened house after darkened house only occasionally interrupted by the throb of a flickering television screen. I manage to get the joint lit and inhale, less deeply than before, but with more sucking success.

"I won't tell if you don't."

I palm the joint and turn around on the bench. A girl, a teenage girl with a nose ring, underdressed in a too-big hooded sweatshirt overtop of black jeans and white low-top Converse running shoes, is sitting in one of the two swings still hanging from the swing set, the other one wrapped around and around its top. She must have been sitting there the entire time. I've managed to extinguish the joint on the edge of the bench and am about to ask her what she means when I see the tiny orange glow of her own joint as she lifts it to her mouth.

"Good luck," I say, standing up, going back the way I came. *Good luck*. What a ridiculous thing to say.

She's busy inhaling, obviously knows what she's doing, only nods.

"You, too," I hear through the dark, and then I'm home.

CHAPTER TWO

"WHAT YOU WANT TO DO IS PROVIDE your father with actual physical reminders of his past. It's not enough to conversationally bring them up—he needs to actually see them, even touch them for himself."

Uncle Donny and I are sitting across the desk from Mrs. Hampton, director of the Alzheimer's ward.

"Right. But…"

Mrs. Hampton raises an eyebrow; Uncle Donny recrosses his legs, right over left this time, looks out the window.

"But he doesn't… I mean, what we talked about—the seventh stage, the severest or advanced stage—the stage you said he's at now. Isn't that when the patient is basically unable to communicate or remember anything?"

"Unfortunately, yes. That's an inevitable part of the disease's progress. And in your father's case, the disease has been unusually aggressive."

"Right. So…"

Mrs. Hampton's eyebrow manages to lift even higher, nearly merging with her hairline. Uncle Donny has got his chin in his hand now, elbow on his crossed knee.

"So what's the point?" I say, more huffily, I know, than I have a right to. Mrs. Hampton and Uncle Donny and all of Dad's other caretakers have been here from the beginning, the entire deterioration countdown. I've been counting, too, but not in person, at least not every day. I don't deserve to be so annoyed. Not at people trying to help, anyway.

"I'm sorry," I say. "I'm just frustrated."

"Of course you are," Mrs. Hampton says. "That's perfectly understandable. Just try to be patient."

I nod. "I'll try."

"Good," she says. "Now. On to other matters. As I'm sure your uncle has made you aware, I think you'll agree that Thames View has been very patient in the matter of—"

"Oh, he agrees," Uncle Donny says, popping up from his chair. "We're both on board with you 110 percent, believe you me. And we both understand what has to be done, absolutely. And pronto, too."

"Well, that's—"

But Uncle Donny has grabbed her hand and is shaking it so vigorously she can't complete her sentence before he's got me by the elbow and has practically dragged me out the door.

"What was that all about?" I say. "What is it you're supposed to have made me understand?"

Uncle Donny swats the air in front of his face like he's being bothered by a pesky mosquito. "If you give that woman half a chance she'll yak your ear right off."

"But what was she talking about?"

"Who knows? A woman like that, she just likes to hear herself talk."

We've already done our Dad visit—watched him be fed; watched him slurp milk with the aid of what's left of his gulping reflex—and are heading toward the front door at the other end of the building when Uncle Donny's hand is in and out of my coat pocket before I know what he's doing. "Take 'em," he says.

I pull out three brand new toothbrushes still in their packaging. "Where did you get these?" I whisper, afraid that he'd somehow managed to lift them from Thames View, afraid that this is the first forgetful sign that he's the next Samson family member on the fast track to assisted living.

"Shopper's," he says. "They were half-price last week, and then this week they were half-price again on top of *that*. Seventy-two cents each before tax. That's like giving them away."

I don't bother informing him that, no matter how extraordinary the discount, I don't really need three toothbrushes in addition to the one I already have; instead, say only, "Thanks."

"I'm telling you, that's like *giving* them away."

I stick the toothbrushes back in my pocket, in the process notice for the first time that Uncle Donny is wearing a cell phone on his belt. Aside from him being cheap enough that he'd be using a tin can and a piece of string at home if he could get away with it, there's no one for him to call and no one to call him.

"What's with that?" I say, tapping the phone with a forefinger.

"It's a phone."

"Yeah, I know what it is. Why do *you* have one?"

"So I can talk to people. Why the hell else would I have one?"

We're almost at the front door when an old woman inching down the connecting corridor with the aid of an aluminum cane smiles at us like we're arriving relatives and not exiting strangers. She's wearing the standard Thames

View Gardens old lady uniform—loose-fitting, matching floral blouse and pants; spotlight-white running shoes; big brown plastic glasses; freshly cut, hairspray-hardened hairdo—but her warm, welcoming face is the energizing upper that I didn't take this morning when I sat down at the kitchen table to work. Maybe caffeine and positive visualization *are* enough to get one through the day. And who knows? Maybe somewhere way back there in his decomposing brain Dad is just as happy as her, we just can't see it. After all, aside from watching the Red Wings and doing lawn work, eating and sleeping were his favourite things to do anyway. Twenty-four hours of both now, and a full-time staff to make sure he never misses a single meal or afternoon nap.

I grin the old lady as good as she gave—I was a dog owner long enough to know that wagging tails beget wagging tails—and while Uncle Donny steps ahead to open the door, the old lady shuffles past; although not before catching me hard across my right shin with a whack of her cane.

"Fuck," I say, hopping on one leg, rubbing my burning shin.

"Hey," Uncle Donny snaps, spinning around at the door. "Watch your mouth." He nods in the direction of the escaping old lady. "These people in here, they don't want to hear language like that." He finally notices me massaging my leg. "What the hell's the matter with you?"

"That woman," I say, pointing. "She…" I stop rubbing, stand up straight, watch her snail away behind one of the hallway doors.

"Yeah? That woman what?"

"Nothing." I must have imagined it. I must have been the one who knocked into her. "Let's just get going."

In the parking lot, on the way to the car, "You've got to remember you're not in Toronto anymore," Uncle Donny says. "This is just a small town, for God's sake. People down here, they don't act the same way as they do up there."

* * *

A CUP OF TEA AND AN EXTRA SWEATER and mind over matter just doesn't matter—I need more heat. By keeping a small space heater going full-blast full-time in the basement, I've gotten the water turned back on without the risk of bursting pipes, but my fingers are stuck underneath my armpits for warmth more than they're on the keyboard of my laptop, and instead of the next sentence, my mind is focused on how much warmer it would be if only I wrote in bed where the heating blanket is. Having determined to forsake my customary morning bennie, however, for the sake of a long list of deeply desirable *nots*—not being itchy irritable all of the time; not suffering tear-inducing insomnia; not having perpetual dry mouth, nausea, and for-no-good-reason nervousness; not, in other words, being a pill-poisoned drug addict—there's no chance of my changing my work habits from the vertical to the horizontal for fear of falling straight asleep. Because being clean also means not feeling instantly energetic and extra-mentally alert and even faintly exhilarated, also for no good reason. Mental health has a price, but I'm determined to pay it.

All of my heroes have been dope friends, so the initial decision to self-medicate wasn't difficult. Besides, woozy booze was always my recreational drug of choice—Dexedrine was for working. For getting down to work sooner. For keeping at the work table longer. For making the imagination click quicker. And it did. And did and did. I've written and published six novels plus two collections of essays in the last fourteen years, all the while being busy with making up for the money that rarely comes from writing literature. But teaching or writing book reviews or doing whatever else for a paycheque never needed pharmaceutical assistance. Never *deserved* pharmaceutical assistance. Art was holy because life clearly was not, and that little pill that washed over my tongue each morning was the consecrated wafer that turned the body and mind of merely tepid me into something burning and bright; just like W.H. Auden and Delmore Schwartz and Jack Kerouac and every other dedicated worker in words who knows that the human spirit needs a little chemical boost if it's ever going to soar where it's supposed to.

But nobody flies for free. When Sara was alive, I could cover the cost, or at least better ignore how expensive the bill was. Living alone for the first time in eighteen years, however, everything that's odd or ugly or unhealthy about yourself is amplified, no one around to distract you and no dutiful couple things to do to soften the crazy corners of your mind. Plus, for almost a year after the funeral I wasn't seriously writing, the first extended period since my mid-twenties that I hadn't been filtering all of that artificial energy through my fingers. Not tap-tapping at my laptop, I turned all of that chemically concentrated attention on myself, a wooly woodpecker in a brightly lit house of mirrors. All dosed up and nowhere to go, I got sweaty panicky waiting for the light to change from red to green. I purposefully bumped into texting-obsessed strangers on the sidewalk I knew didn't see me coming. I counted heartbeats at night instead of sheep. (Not that there was much of a chance of my getting an over-abundance of rest anyway—without a dog at the end of the bed cramping your feet and a woman to fight with over the blankets, a bed can be a very uncomfortable place.) When

I got into a shouting match with a street person who, I was sure, called me an asshole when I said I didn't have any spare change, I knew it was time to get help.

Surprisingly, my biggest worry—missing the creative kick of the morning's first black beauty—hasn't been a problem. With enough Mountain Dew and a good night's sleep behind me, the words have found their way onto the page and the pages have been adding up. I'm a hundred pages deep into *Lives of the Poets (with Guitars)* and the only thing I'm lacking right now is my record player and LPs back in Toronto and enough heat to unthaw my fingertips. If only heating blankets were as portable as turntables.

I get up from the kitchen table and head to the basement. My dad had—has—everything the do-it-yourselfer could want: every tool, every spare part, every kind of nail, screw, and washer, each of the latter kept in individual glass baby food jars, their lids nailed to the underside of a ten-foot-long suspended two-by-four for easy see-through identification. Let's see if he has an extension cord. Of course he does—of course he has two: a six-footer and an eighteen-footer.

Upstairs, I pull the heating blanket off the bed and attach it to the shorter extension cord and then plug the longer one into it. Back in the kitchen, with the connected cords plugged into the outlet, I drape the blanket around me like a cape and sit back down at my makeshift kitchen-table desk. Immediately, I feel waves of electric heat washing over my frozen joints and shivering skin. I decide to give my new furnace a test ride—rise and go to the refrigerator and get a can of Mountain Dew, as cozy as could be.

I pop the tab, take a bubbly slurp. Okay. Tonight's topic: Sister Rosetta Tharpe. Let's get down to work.

* * *

"WELL, I'LL BE A SONOFAGUN," Steady Eddie says, nearly scooping me off my feet with a short but rib-bending bear hug. "What's going on, man?"

Before I have a chance to answer, a photograph is whipped from his wallet to my hand. Before I have time to do more than register that it's a picture of a baby, "Check it out, man. What do you think?"

It's a baby all right: bald, pasty, bored-looking. The same as every other baby I've ever seen. But it must be Eddie's latest—he's the same age as me, forty-four, and a father four (or is it five?) times over already—so I reel off the expected bromides: *Wow. Good looking kid. It looks like you. Congratulations.*

Steady Eddie takes back the picture, shakes his head while returning it to his wallet. "Gavin says him and Cheryl might get back together someday. Jimmy—that's the kid's name—wasn't six months old when she told Gavin she didn't want to be tied down anymore, she needed some space. Space, shit. She just wants to party every night like she did before they started shacking up." He's still shaking his head while getting a couple bottles of Labatt Blue from the beer fridge in the garage where we're standing. "I just feel bad for the baby, that's all. Gavin's a good kid, don't get me wrong, but useless as tits on a nun. Kid couldn't spell *cat* if you spotted him the *c* and the *t*." He cracks open our beers with an opener attached to the symphony of keys and mini-screwdrivers and pocket knives clanking from his belt.

I take my beer. "That's rough for Gavin," I say, "but what does his love life have to do with your new son?"

Steady Eddie giggles, tips his bottle, giggles some more. "Jimmy's not *my* son, man, he's Gavin's. Jimmy's my grandson."

I do the math because it's impossible—impossible that I went to school with someone who's a grandfather—but the numbers, unfortunately, add up. Gavin was born the day before our high-school band, The Tyrants, was supposed to play the Christmas assembly, and I was sure we'd have to cancel because our drummer, Steady Eddie, would be an all-of-a-sudden eighteen-year-old father. When I'd called his house, though, the Steady One himself had answered. "No sweat, man, Pam won't be going home with the baby until Saturday. I'll see you tomorrow. I gotta go. Tammy's here." Tammy was Eddie's newest girlfriend, the one who hadn't just borne him a son.

I do what's expected of me, raise my bottle and toast Eddie's good news. He clinks me back and it's official, we're both old farts.

"How's your dad doing?" he says.

I haven't seen or even talked to Eddie since my mother's funeral—Eddie was steady with the 4/4 backbeat, not so much with cracking the books, so after I left for university and Eddie stayed behind to work the assembly line and make more babies, ours became a Chatham friendship, alive when I'm here, dead when I'm in T.O.

"He's all right," I say. "Considering."

Eddie nods, drinks his beer. He knows about my dad's disease just like I know about his dad dying of colon cancer. People from Chatham may not subscribe to *Harper's* or listen to BBC World News, but they know what's important, like who's sick, dead, or dying in Chatham. Or at least have an uncle who's sure to keep them up to date.

"Hey, check this out," Eddie says, going to the wall to admire the most recent addition to the posters and pictures covering the inside of his garage. Eddie's garage is equipped just like my dad's: an old fridge for beer, a mounted

23

television set for sports, a museum of hockey player memorabilia covering whatever wall space isn't taken up with hanging rakes, shovels, and other yard maintenance equipment. And when the weather is nice, and with the car parked in the driveway and the garage door opened wide, several lawn chairs for watching both the Blue Jays game on TV and the much less interesting, non-televised world play its own games out on the sidewalk and in the street.

"I got it at Joe Louis last month when I took Billy with me to see the Wings and Stars. Don't even ask me how much it cost."

It's what I guess you'd call a painting—sort of the sporting equivalent of an orange tiger leaping across a black velvet canvas—a sight-impaired oil painter's impression of every Red Wings captain of the last seventy-five years holding aloft the Stanley Cup, whether they actually did so or not. Steady Eddie giggles, points out the artist's version of Dennis Polonich, which more closely resembles Horshack from *Welcome Back, Kotter* than the diminutive late-'70s Red Wing dynamo. "Old Polo, eh?" Eddie says. "What a little prick he could be, couldn't he?"

"Nasty with his stick, that's for sure."

"Oh, yeah, cut your heart out with that thing."

"Could play some, too, though."

"Oh, don't kid yourself, you know he could."

We both drink and pay silent homage to Polo, one of the few battling bright spots for a string of perpetually lousy Red Wings teams during the 1970s, when the team still played out of the ratty old Olympia. Whenever my dad would take me to a game we'd park in Windsor and take the tunnel bus over to dangerous downtown Detroit. As soon as we were off the bus and walking the few hundred feet to the arena, my dad would take my hand. I would have been too embarrassed to let him do it at home, but I always held on tight until we were safe inside the rink. Then, when everything would be all right—the sound of program hawkers, the smell of hot dogs, the view of the zamboni circling the ice—I'd drop his hand and be the big boy again that I was at home.

Steady Eddie sits down on a riding lawnmower; I lean against the wall, between an action shot of Steve Yzerman and a gas-powered leaf blower. The lawn chairs are months away from being broken out. Eddie must have been out somewhere just before I dropped by; the car engine periodically pings above the whir of the winter wind outside.

"You still at ... ?" I say, hoping Eddie will finish my sentence for me. In the '80s, when I left for U of T and Eddie went to work at Fram, the big factories in town—International Harvester, Rockwell, Fram—were still pumping out trucks and car parts and paying out a good wage to just about anyone who was willing to work the line. Over the last twenty-five years, though, most of the larger companies having permanently emigrated south, everyone in town has been pawing over the same handful of decent-paying positions, mostly at parts operations run as small branch plants by companies outside Canada. Every time I talk to Eddie it seems as if he's working somewhere different.

"Campton's?" he says. "In Dresden?"

That sounds about right. "Yeah, Campton's."

"Shit, no, they shut that place down last year. I'm over where your dad used to be, at Sieman's, in Tilbury."

Where my dad retired from after fourteen years. After twenty-one years at Ontario Steel, five years at Chrysler, and three years at Navistar. At least in that his timing was good: four well-paying factory jobs in forty-three years is a pretty impressive run. Not too many grade nine dropouts today can hope to end up paying off their mortgage by the time they're fifty while still having steadily saved up enough Friday paycheques to help put their kid through university. My dad did.

"Does it look good?" I say. Not *Does the work look good?* or *Are the people you work with good people?* or even *Is the pay good?* But does it look good that they'll keep you on so that you can continue buying shitty art for your garage walls and sinfully overpriced blue jeans for your ungrateful children and, more than likely, diapers and baby food and rattles for the spurious spawn of your mouth-breathing eldest son. Creative fulfillment and a positive, nurturing work environment aren't Chatham workplace priorities. Paying your bills and feeding and clothing your children are.

Eddie shrugs; I nod into my beer.

"Hey, how's the old—" Eddie says, making a scribbling motion with his non-beer-holding hand "—going?"

"It's all right."

"You got a new one coming out?"

"I'm working on it."

"Good stuff. I told you, I'm saving up all your books for my retirement. Gonna get me a hammock and read 'em all in a row swinging with a brew beside me in the backyard. That's the way to do it, right?"

I smile, sip. Eddie will never read any of my books and that's just fine. Eddie buys my books—one of the few people in Chatham I know who does—and always gets me to inscribe them whenever I next see him. I appreciate the online sale of one novel dutifully purchased every two years or so, but more than that, I appreciate that Eddie is genuinely happy that I'm happy, am pleased that he's authentically pleased that someone he actually knows ended up doing what they wanted to do with their life. If he couldn't play defence in the National Hockey League, at least I get to sit on my ass all day making stuff up. Artsy-fartsy deflected glory is still deflected glory.

"Hey, that reminds me," he says. "I got the new one inside. Let me go in and get it so you can put your ol' John Hancock on it."

"Sure."

Before I have time to tour in its entirety even a single wall of Eddie' tacked-up museum—Detroit players mostly, but the occasionally deserving non-Red Wing as well (mostly long-retired opposition tough guys who could also put the puck in the net, like Terry O'Reilly and Clark Gillies and Cam Neely), Eddie is back in the garage with a pen and a copy of my latest novel still encased in its shipping box. Using a pen knife from his key chain to cut it free, "I figured I'd just keep it in here until you were back in town. That way it wouldn't get dirty or anything."

"Makes sense," I say, taking the liberated book and the pen.

Eddie watches me while I stand there trying to think of something profound or funny or at least not utterly banal to write on the title page. It's always easier to sign a book for a stranger than for a friend. A guy who says he came to your reading from Hamilton immediately gets *To Fred from the Hammer, Best, Sam Samson*, but someone who watched you get beat up in the parking lot of McDonald's after the Sadie Hawkins dance when you were seventeen and who encouraged you afterward to super-size your meal because you fucking deserve it, man, you never stopped throwing those fucking haymakers even when you were bleeding like a stuck fucking pig, is harder to be so cocky casual with.

To Steady Eddie, I finally write.
Health and Happiness.
Sam.

Eddie takes back his book, immediately reads what's there. And giggles. If a 235-pound giggling man doesn't make you smile, maybe it's time to consider changing your medication. Closing the book and setting it on top of the fridge, "Where are you off to?" he says. "You got time for one more?"

Uncle Donny is picking me up at home in an hour to take me to Thames View so that we can pretend that Dad is glad we've come to visit.

"Why not?" I say.

"To health and happiness," Eddie says.

We clink our bottles, and Eddie's car joins in with a ping.

* * *

"YOU SURE IT'S PLUGGED IN?" Uncle Donny says.

"Of course it's plugged in."

"You'd be surprised how many times I thought my lawn mower was busted and all the time it was just out of gas."

Believe me, no, I wouldn't. I keep pushing buttons on the remote until eventually the television speaks its first words. I turn down the volume—that was Thames View's only condition of our bringing in a small portable television for Dad to stare at in the evenings: that we keep the volume low, not so much in consideration of the other equally oblivious patients as of their assembled visitors.

The TV was my idea. Dad without a hockey game on in the background doesn't seem like Dad. It's three o'clock in the afternoon, though, and the evening's first faceoff is four hours away, so I flip. The tiny television set is resting on a metal tray attached to the far end of the bed, Uncle Donny and I sitting on chairs on either side of Dad. Neither of us says a word as one blah-blah-blah channel replaces the next. I stop at a black and white war documentary, Korean War variety, it looks like. "How about this?" I say.

Uncle Donny shrugs. "I don't know. If it's not about Nazis, I just don't find history shows very interesting." Just so there's no confusion about where he stands on the issue of the National Socialist Party of Germany, however, "Those guys were bad news, you know," he adds.

"I've heard that."

"Bad, bad news, believe you me."

There's a soccer game on TSN, but as disparate a lot as we are, the Samson men are united at least in their unspoken but no less firmly held belief that any activity in which men wear shorts but are not permitted to body check one another is not a real sport. Uncle Donny insists I leave it on the match, however, until all of tonight's hockey games and their times are finished scrolling across the bottom of the screen.

I recommence clicking. There's a combination nature/science program on one of the educational stations, and this time I don't ask, just leave it. Uncle Donny announces he's got to make a phone call, and before I can ask him who he has to suddenly speak to, he's gone. The concept of Uncle Donny having a girlfriend crosses my mind and lingers there like a bad smell in the refrigerator that no amount of disinfectant can get rid of. Dad's eyes, if not his attention, are on the TV screen, and I join him.

Apparently there's a parrot that's been taught a vocabulary of over a hundred words, inspiring several scientists with thick glasses and thinning hair to speculate on the giddy possibility of a bird capable of authentic human conversation. Just what we need: another nattering species to bore us with what they think, with what they're feeling, with who they really, really are deep down inside.

I turn off the TV. Dad stares at the dead screen with as much interest as when it was alive. Maybe not parrots, but people, certainly, are supposed to talk. Most of the time you wish they wouldn't, most of the time they haven't got a single thing to say, but that's what they're supposed to do. Sometimes, when he could still remember my phone number, Dad would call me in Toronto and ask me who he was. The first time he did it, I thought he was joking, said, *That's the million dollar question, isn't it?* When the line went quiet, *Dad*, I said. *Are you still there?*

You've got the wrong number, he answered, and hung up.

* * *

TWO HOURS OF UNCLE DONNY TALKING interspersed with two hours of Dad not talking followed by three hours of Mountain Dew-abetted writing—I need this. Before I put match to joint, though, I decide to take my toking outside, the fresh air on my face probably as good for cooling down my over-busy brain as the warm smoke in my lungs. I peel off the heating blanket and put on my coat and hope that the parkette is empty. It's 11:30 on a Thursday night in January in Chatham. Of course it'll be empty.

And it is, for as long as it takes me to light up and cough right back out what I just breathed in.

From behind me, "It's probably best if we don't wake the grown-ups."

I turn around on the bench but don't need to, immediately recognize the voice from last time. "How do you know I'm not a grown-up?"

The girl inhales, holds it, emits a perfect stream of smoke. "Just a hunch," she says.

Since she doesn't appear to be going anywhere and it seems silly to turn around and pretend she's not there, I get up from the bench and pretend to admire the night sky. I casually take another toke; not so casually hack my way to a raw windpipe and two watery eyes.

"Not much danger of you becoming a pothead, is there?" the girl says.

Still coughing, "I"—right forefinger raised, just a moment, please, while I—"don't usually"—bent over, hands on both knees now, tears clogging both eyes—"smoke"—

"Marijuana. Yeah, I can see that." She gives me a moment to stand upright and wipe my eyes dry. My joint has gone dead. On the plus side, no one has turned on their porch light or set their Rottweiler on us. Not yet, anyway. "Why bother, then?"

I attempt to relight the joint while considering her question, but the wind is always one stifling step ahead. I give up and stand there in the cold blowy night with the extinguished joint in one hand and the useless lighter in the other. "Self-improvement," I say.

The girl makes a perfect pucker, sucks in another lung-ful of dopey smoke. "I've never heard of anyone taking up pot smoking to better themself."

"There are a lot worse things to do to yourself, believe me."

"Now that's the kind of thing I like to hear from an adult. You should talk to my shrink."

Shrink? The girl's—what? Seventeen? Eighteen? Besides, people in Chatham don't go to psychiatrists. When I was her age, psychiatrists were who actors in Woody Allen movies visited, or maybe characters in Robertson Davies novels set in Toronto.

"He doesn't approve?"

"*She* says I have an unhealthy propensity to self-medicate."

"Tell her she should be proud of you. Tell her self-medication shows initiative."

The girl laughs. "Do you want me to show you?" she says.

Hold on a minute—show me what, exactly? Nice smile or not, unusually precocious or not, if Steady Eddie can be a grandfather, I could be this girl's father.

"I should head inside," I say, thumbing in the direction of the house, just to make sure it's absolutely clear I've got somewhere I should be—and, by extension, so does she.

"I wasn't offering to fuck you," she says.

"No, no, I know. No. God, no." Out comes the thumb again. "I just—"

"Show you how to get high," she says. "Do you want me to show you how to get high."

"Right. Of course. Right."

"So?"

"So … yeah, sure. Thanks."

The girl pats the empty swing beside her. Not like a brazen temptress, more like a patient owner with a willing but witless puppy. "Watch," she says, returning the joint to her mouth. "Breathe in the smoke like this." Which she does—like a flight attendant patiently instructing her passengers how to fasten their seatbelts—before calmly pausing and then gently inhaling what's left. "And then you swallow it as best as you can, just like I did, and that's that." She hands me her joint. "Now you try."

As a last resort, read the instructions—or get someone who knows what they're doing to show you how. By my second attempt, I swear I'm stoned. As if on cue, it starts to snow: large, lazy flakes fluttering, falling, softly landing. The girl, swinging in her seat, wordlessly hands me back the joint and I puff and pass it back to her. I watch the snowflakes—falling harder now and blowing sideways in the escalating wind—illuminated underneath the street light.

"A Petri dish of hysteria," I say.

The girl looks at me, but I point until she sees what I'm staring at, joins me in looking at the frantic activity beneath the light.

A long moment later, "You're right," she says.

I nod, benignly accepting the compliment. Poetry isn't big words saying not all that much, isn't flowery fakery stitched together to remind the reader to LOOK AT ME, I'M A POET. Isn't supposed to be, anyway. Poetry is a magnifying glass that makes the stuff that makes up the world come closer so that the reader can see it better and know it better and live it better. Even the bad stuff. Maybe even especially the bad stuff.

"Did you just make that up?" the girl says.

"Make what up?" I'd forgotten I wasn't alone.

"'Petri dish of hysteria.'"

"Oh. No."

"Oh," the girl says, obviously disappointed. She takes her hands off the chains of the swing and folds her arms across her chest.

"It's from my first book."

The girl stops swinging; unfolds her arms and turns to me. "You wrote a book?"

"I wrote *that* book in … 1997. At least that's when it was published."

"You've written more than one book?"

Even taking into consideration the brain-baked banter that ordinarily goes along with what we're doing, this is a little too mush-headed much. "I write novels," I say.

Not *I'm a novelist* or *I'm a writer* because you're only a writer when you're actually sitting in front of your computer writing. Only amateurs and over-prized professionals call themselves *writers*. Right now I'm a forty-four year old man sitting on a swing set getting stoned with a teenage girl.

"If you're a writer … why are you here?" she says.

Here means *Chatham*. "I was born here. I grew up here. This was my parents' house."

"You're just visiting."

Visiting. Well, that's the idea, anyway. "Sort of. It's complicated."

"I didn't think anything about Chatham was complicated."

That's *all* Chatham is, I want to say. That's all anyone's hometown is. But that's what novels are for, scarcely saying in 80,000 words what everyone else thinks can be summed up in eight.

"You don't seem like"—or look like or sound like—"you're from Chatham," I say.

"My father came here for his work last year." Nose nearly in the air, "I'm from Toronto."

"Really? Which part?"

"Oakville."

Which probably does impress her Chatham classmates who don't know enough to know that Oakville has about as much to do with Toronto as Bogota, New Jersey has to do with New York City. But let her have her hometown haughtiness. Growing up in a small town is bad enough—being parachuted in at eighteen and knowing what you're missing is probably worse. "What does your dad do?"

"I have no idea." The girl appears almost proud of her ignorance.

"You know your father came to Chatham for his work but you don't know what he does?"

"I didn't say that. He's a lawyer. I said I don't know what he does. Or care."

Pass—Ms. Toronto's family fissures aren't my row to hoe, I've got my own domestic dramas to tend to—so please just pass me that jay, okay? Which she does, which I dooby do correctly the first time around this time, which presently nicely negates all of this all-of-a-sudden logic. Fuzzy-headed and nicely thoroughly fuddled once again, look at that: snow. It was there the entire time we were talking and I hadn't noticed. Marijuana makes you notice things. I hadn't noticed that before.

"What are you ... now?" The girl has taken back the spliff and is as obviously spaced as I am.

"Exactly," I answer.

"No, I mean, what ... what are you writing now? A new novel?"

"No, not a novel." The girl waits, isn't going to let it go, I can tell. "A music book. A book about music."

"What—like your personal Top Ten or something?"

I give her as brief a brief as possible, to which she responds, "Awesome," sounding for the first time like an actual teenager. She pulls her iPod out of the pouch of her hoodie and immediately begins thumbing it. "You've got to check this out, it's total dope. Do you know Maps? They're from the UK. They're kind of like Spiritualized and Galaxie 500 but so much better." She finds what she's looking for and hands me the iPod. "Check this out."

I stand up. "I better not. It's getting cold."

"Now you're suddenly cold?"

I'm high enough, I almost tell her the truth. That just like you should never mix alcohol and night-time swimming, I never mingle a good buzz with bad music. Or even music I don't know for sure is good. And certainly not music recommended, no matter how heartily, by a transplanted teenager from Oakville. "I'm a grown-up, remember? I'm just being a responsible adult."

"Whatever," the girl says, jamming her iPod back into her pouch and pulling on her hood and walking away from the swing set.

"Thanks for the lesson," I call out after her.

Still walking, and without bothering to turn around, the girl raises a statuary hand goodbye until I finally make out that she's not, has been giving me the finger the entire time.

I don't know why, but even when I'm in the house, even later when I'm in bed, I'm smiling.

CHAPTER THREE

IT'S NOT THE GIRL'S FAULT. Unless you were born here, why else would you care? Although *care* isn't quite the right word. *Obsess*—that's closer—although even that implies some sort of conscious act of concern when what it really comes down to is not being able to forget.

It's the fields—still rich and alive and giving. Corn, beans, squash, peppers, tomatoes, cucumbers, radishes, potatoes: every spring planted and every summer harvested and always on local dinner tables all year long regardless of what the newspapers or the television insist is this season's big business boom or bust. Bank loans and broken tractors and bad weather, but still the land. And sundown of an August evening—the hot, humid air finally cooling, the shadows of the tall corn stalks stretching, the exhausting day's work almost over—the peace of the land, too, the sun-burnt earth's long, soft exhale.

It's the town. Battered, yes—economic winds blowing in from who knows where or why knocking down factory walls and boarding up storefronts and pushing people out of their homes—but not broken. The barber where your father and then you got your hair cut. The grocery store that's still there, where it's always been. The school that seemed so big when you were young but so small now that you're not. The bar where everyone buys their first beer. The church where you learned what and what not to believe. The tattoo parlour you were warned to stay away from. The post office and the laundromat and the library. The Legion Hall, the Bingo, the Dairy Queen. The water tower with the town's—your town's—name written across it. The grain mill that's sat silent for years now. The same cemetery where everyone buries their dead. The hockey arena and the baseball fields and the parks. The hospital where your mother was pronounced dead; where you had your tonsils removed. The houses that are the homes that are the families that are the neighbourhoods that make a town a town, any town. And the river that runs through all of it, for as long as there's been a town.

It's the people. The teacher who taught you how to read. The dentist who helped make your teeth grow straight. The coach who made you try harder. The old man who gave you your first job, cutting his lawn for three whole dollars. The woman whose kids you babysat. The doctor who made you feel better. The old lady next door whose driveway you shoveled. Your first best friend. Your first ever kiss. Your first broken heart. First lies, last goodbyes, endless summer holidays. The cats and dogs and birds and fish you named and loved and lost but never forgot. The brothers and sisters and aunts and uncles and cousins and grandparents whose faces and even names you sometimes forget but who will always have your eyes, just like you'll always have their cheekbones. Your mum and your dad.

Whether you stay and raise a family and die here. Whether you grow up and leave and never come back. Whether you call it home or say it's just where you were born or don't say anything at all, not even to yourself. It's where you're from. It's your hometown. It's you. Even if you're from Oakville. Even if you're from Chatham.

*　*　*

NO FRILLS IS CLOSE ENOUGH TO Buttercup Village that I can walk there, a rare indigenous pleasure. I need food and Mountain Dew, but also cardboard boxes. It's time to decide what's a cherished family memento and what's garbage. Aside from seeing more of Dad, putting the house up for sale is the real reason I'm here. Which doesn't make it feel any more real.

Around the same time that Uncle Donny started bringing up nursing homes—him staying over at Dad's place every night by this point, the nurse we'd hired to help out coming by virtually every day—Sara was killed. I was involved in the move to Thames View, I still came home to visit, but I wasn't there. Not really. A change may be as good as a rest, but not when numbing bereavement is periodically interrupted for disheartening parental concern. I wasn't the son I should have been, I know that, and for making Dad's move to Thames View as smooth as it was and for taking care of him before it came to that, I owe Uncle Donny. He may talk too much sometimes and buy things he doesn't need because a deal is simply too good to resist, but he's family—except for several cousins I probably wouldn't recognize if I passed them on the sidewalk, all the family I've got left.

"Sam?"

I'm slouching at a traffic light and stoop to peer inside the driver's side of the car that's stopped beside me. A black BMW driven by an attractive blonde woman in big sunglasses: not anyone I would know in Toronto, forget about here. A dedicated reader? Unlikely in Toronto, out of the question here. I try to remember if there's anyone in Chatham I owe money to that I'd forgotten about.

The woman grins and takes off her sunglasses, appears to be enjoying my cluelessness. "It's Rachel," she says.

I smile back, pretending to finally be in on the joke, but not any nearer to actually knowing who she is. I'm almost ready to admit defeat when she says, "Rachel Turnbal."

Impossible. Simply impossible. But then my brain gets busy, begins adding width and weight to the thin arm holding the sunglasses; appends an additional couple chins to the one that's already there; discerns a neck where there once was just shoulders directly melded to head; registers the kind, lettuce-green eyes that were always Rachel's. Rachel Turnbal's.

'My God," I say, "I'm sorry, it's been ... How are you?"

"Do you want a ride?"

"That would be great."

Waiting as long as the honking traffic behind her will allow, "Why don't you get in, then?"

I jog around to the other side of the car and get in.

"Where are you going?" Rachel says, putting the Beemer in gear and rocketing us off.

"No Frills."

"No Frills it is." Which, after she shifts gears again, will be in approximately seven seconds the way we're flying down Lacroix Street. I double-check to see if my seat belt is fastened.

By determinedly avoiding looking at her, I'm sure I'm only confirming her suspicion of what I'm thinking, which she seems content to let me do. She probably gets this a lot. How many people, after all, get to become another person?

"So the famous writer comes back home. The famous novelist."

Unbelievable: someone from my graduating high-school class of nearly a quarter-century ago has actually read my books. With an exaggerated grimace like she's just turned around at the bar and spilt her drink all down the front of my shirt, "Although I'm afraid I haven't read any of them," she says. "I'm a public school teacher. I haven't had time to read something I didn't have to teach in ten years, and when I do finally have some time to myself, the last thing I want to do is look at words on a page. I didn't actually know you were a writer until I saw that article in the *Chatham Daily News* the last time you were here, when you were doing something at one of the high schools, I think. What was that, a couple of years ago now?"

"About that," I say. "Actually, I was at CCI." CCI is Chatham Collegiate Institute, our alma mater. "No one left from our time, though. Except for Mrs. Adams."

"Mrs. Adams: Mrs. Creepy Crawler." Mrs. Adams was CCI's biology teacher when Rachel was my grade ten lab partner. We dissected our first worms together.

"She looked pretty good," I say. "About as good as she did back then, at least."

"And here we are," Rachel says, and she isn't kidding, whipping into the No Frills parking lot on what feels like two wheels before stopping directly out front of its doors. "I'd love to get caught up, but I was supposed to be at my parents' house for dinner half an hour ago."

"No problem," I say.

I'm standing on the frozen blacktop with my hands in my coat pockets when Rachel says, "I suppose you heard they're trying to shut down CCI?"

"No. I hadn't." Uncle Donny's field of gossip extends only as far as personal misfortune and the flagrant misuse of taxpayer money. "Why would they want to do that?"

"Oh, the usual reason—money. Here." She reaches into her purse and produces a pen and a scrap of paper which she scribbles on, pen cap in mouth, before handing it to me. "Call me if you're interested in being on a committee some of the alumni and parents are organizing to try and save it. It mostly means putting your name on petitions, but the more people involved the better."

"Sure."

"Oh, what am I thinking? You're probably only in town for just a few days, right? Are you visiting your parents or something like that?"

"No, I—Yeah, something like that. Anyway, I'm going to be around for awhile."

"That's great. I guess." Rachel roars the engine. "Anyway, good to see you again, Sam. And call me if you're interested."

A horn beeps behind her, and Rachel waves goodbye. I fold her phone number into my wallet and head inside No Frills. I have no idea how many boxes I'm going to need. I guess I'll just start with a few and see what happens from there.

*　　*　　*

IF THE WEATHER IS PLEASANT, if your health is perfect, if you happen to discover a ten dollar bill you didn't know you had in the back pocket of a pair of jeans you rarely wear, it's possible to pretend that drugs, alcohol, and loud, loud music aren't the only things capable of making a person happy. Just one humidity-soiled, freshly-donned clean shirt, though; just one slightly achy arthritic knuckle or even a more-irritating-than-actually-painful midwinter sore throat, however, and a nose gets white-dust itchy and lips get hoochy dry. Ditto when you've spent nearly three hours going though your parents' closets and drawers and a single metal filing cabinet and can't come up with anything more memento memorable than four years' worth of elementary-school report cards (mine), a still-polished pair of first baby shoes (also mine), the crappy Christmas gifts we'd annually mangle out of pipe cleaners and white glue and construction paper in grade school that I'd give to my mother and that she actually kept, and the single letter I sent home during first-year university telling them how much I loved both it and Toronto and how much I appreciated their helping me get there, Talk to you soon, Sam.

Wait: one more thing: a driftwood-encased dual clock and thermometer set that my dad received from Siemens on the day he retired. At first it had sat on one of my mother's doily-topped side tables in the living room, but the clock always ran a couple of minutes slow, so Dad eventually banished it to the top shelf of their bedroom closet. All together, I've filled less than half of one small cardboard box. It's a good thing I don't know any drug dealers in Chatham. I get a beer from the fridge and a joint from my stash and exchange the heating blanket for my coat. It's just after midnight—maybe I'll get lucky and be accosted by a roving gang of crack dealers.

Carefully recalling what I'd been taught, I manage to light up on the first try. I toke and sip and lean back on the bench and wait for the smoke and the suds to tag team my brain. In the time it takes a jigsaw-piece cloud to make the frozen moon disappear, I'm high, or, at any rate, as high as marijuana can get you. They should call smoking pot getting *low*. But at least I'm not normal, at least I'm below see-yourself level.

Besides, apparently that's the source of my entire substance abuse problem. When I'm up—whether because writing-well exhilarated or plain old chemically enhanced overstimulated (or a bit of both because the one doesn't usually wander too far from home without the other)—I want to stay up. And when staying up inevitably leads to not just good work done or giddy times had, but involuntarily clenched molars and pin-wheeling pupils and the inability to sleep, eat, or sit still for longer than a single accelerated heart beat, maybe it's time to consider professional help. People who quit using drugs seldom talk about the real reason they became addicts. It wasn't your troubled childhood or the pressures of modern society or the depraved, enabling company you kept—it's because being high finally feels like being alive. Unfortunately, being alive too much or for too long will kill you. Or make you wish that you were dead.

Thankfully, when I finally decided I needed help, I got the help I needed. Like anything you really require, though, it wasn't a matter of simply asking for it. You never get what you ask for—you always have to force someone to give it to you.

"And how long have you been self-administering"—the counsellor pressed a forefinger to the three-page questionnaire I'd filled out while waiting for my two PM appointment—"dextroamphetamine sulfate?" I could tell by the way he'd studied the word that he had no idea what it was.

"It's basically a pharmaceutical-quality stimulant," I said.

Without lifting his eyes from the questionnaire, "I'm familiar with"—finger on the page again—"dextroamphetamine sulfate." Flipping back to the first page, "And you've just turned forty-four?"

"Yes," I said, although, No, I wanted to say—I've just admitted to a complete stranger that I'm addicted to speed, but I lied about my age, I'm secretly really forty-five.

"And you're a teacher, I see."

"Right."

This fact seemed to interest him; enough so, anyway, that he looked up at me from the piece of paper. He was tennis club thin and probably no more than fifty, but, I noticed for the first time, sporting not only a surgically implanted weave and a tanning-booth baked glow, but braces. A fifty-year-old man with braces. *This* was the person who was going to help me get my life back? *I* was the one who needed professional help?

"And where do you teach?"

"U of T. Continuing Studies. It's just a couple of hours a week."

The counsellor slowly, almost imperceptibly, shook his head—although not, I thought, without dimly smiling—and wrote something in the margins of the questionnaire, pleased, it seemed, to have discovered the source of my problem in the first five minutes of our meeting. "And do you think that two hours a week of fulfilling work is enough to satisfactorily occupy yourself as an educator?"

"I'm not a teacher," I said. "I mean, I am, but I'm busy with other things as well. Believe me, work isn't my problem. It's probably the only thing in my life that *isn't* a problem."

He scanned the questionnaire, undoubtedly looking to determine what precisely these other things were. "Do you mind me asking you how you're able to support yourself on two hours of part-time teaching?"

I'd hoped it wouldn't come to this. Neither the present status of my bank account nor the insurance settlement I'd received upon Sara's death that I used to pay off our mortgage was his or anybody else's business. *Sara* wasn't his or anyone else's business. Under MARITAL STATUS on the questionnaire, I'd checked the box marked SINGLE.

"I write books," I said. "A large portion of my income comes from the books I write."

The counsellor leaned back in his chair, chin in hand, and nodded—leisurely, indulgently—not unlike an insane asylum overseer humouring an inmate claiming to be Jesus Christ.

"I mean," I continued, "the money's not all from the books themselves. There are grants, readings fees, public lending rights money, things like that."

Another exaggeratedly benevolent nod. "These books that you speak of: are these books that you would *like* to write someday?"

Now I was getting angry, and not just because I was more than a little cranky from not having slept more than three consecutive hours in who knew how long. "No, these are actual books that I've actually written." I hated to be an artsy shit about it, but, "There are six novels and two collections of essays."

"I see," he said. "And these 'books'"—he made scare quotes with his fingers, he literally, physically made scare quotes—"would you say that, perhaps, some of your struggles with dextro—"

"Speed. I've got a problem with speed."

The counsellor paused, allowing me time, it was clear, to compose myself. "That perhaps some of your struggles are attributable to your not being published? It wouldn't, after all, be the first time that an aspiring author—"

"I am published."

"Self-published, do you mean?"

"No, published—*published*—as in published by a publisher."

Fingers in the air again, "These 'publishers' that you speak of—"

"Oh, for Christ sake, Google me."

"I beg your pardon?"

"I'm serious, turn on your computer and just punch in my name."

"Mr. Samson, please lower your voice."

"Do it, just punch in my name."

"Mr. Samson, I'll ask you again to please lower your voice."

"Will you listen to me? I'm telling you, Google me."

"Mr. Samson, I won't ask you again."

"For Godsake, I've got my own fucking website!"

By the time the security guard arrived, I'd managed to find the ON switch at the back of the computer and was waiting for Windows to load, www.SamSamson.ca just one click away.

Luckily, instead of being banned from the premises, I was "referred" (scare quotes mine) to another counsellor—a big Swedish woman this time—who listened when I spoke and helped me to admit that perhaps I'd reached the point in my life when the going up so high wasn't quite worth the coming down so low. She also gave me expert guidance and continued general support to assist me in edging off the dexys little by little, day by day, until within two months, the strongest chemical I was putting inside my body was Mountain Dew, the most caffeine-charged soda pop known to humankind, the edgy energy it delivers with every bubbly sip just the jumpy jump-start my rev-ving-up system needs. Thank God for the Dew and my big Swedish counsellor.

My beer is gone and the wind has picked up and my joint keeps going out; and besides, no matter how faithfully I follow the girl's instructions, even when I can manage to keep it lit, I can't smuggle enough smoke into my lungs to make me feel any more stoned than as if I'd just woken up from a very long, too long, nap. I empty the sudsy remains of the beer bottle onto the snow and realize that I'm just killing time, am hoping that the girl is going to join me.

I storm into the house, angry at myself, disappointed with myself, something.

* * *

I SPEND MOST OF THE MORNING addressing e-mails that can't go unanswered any longer; then, because Uncle Donny won't be here to pick me up until noon, waste nearly an hour Googling myself, in the process discovering absolutely nothing about me that I didn't already know. Anyway, that's what best friends are for, lovers are for, Sara is for. Was for. The final grammar lesson that no one wants to learn: the difference between *is* and *was* isn't just a different vowel with an extra consonant thrown in.

My big Swedish counsellor was only wrong about one thing. When she advised me to compile a list of all those friends who might, by virtue of their own nasty habits, impede my desire to remain dexy-free, I told her it wouldn't be necessary, I didn't have any friends. When she replied, more kindly than accusingly, that that seemed unlikely, I realized it would be easier to concede she was right. But I was telling the truth. For the longest time, I didn't need any friends. For the longest time, I had Sara.

Dearest Emily Dickinson opined "The Soul selects her own Society/Then shuts the Door," and the old girl never wrote righter. I had people I knew when we met and Sara had plenty of the same, but over the course of twenty years together our society naturally selected down to just us. Sara and me. Me and Sara. Sara and Sam. Sam and Sara. Us.

People we hadn't seen for months—nice people, good people, other writers or people in publishing I knew; people who worked with Sara in fundraising at the OSPCA—would run into one or the other of us and say, "We never see you guys anymore. We really need to get together." And e-mail addresses would be verified and phone calls would be promised and another few months would go by and it would still be just Sara and Sam, Sam and Sara. It wasn't misanthropy; we never fell out with anyone; it was never anything we planned on happening. But even when we fought, we knew there was only us. We'd snap, we'd snarl, we'd scream at each other, but it was almost like arguing with yourself—as if, until a soft word or firm embrace finally stopped the shouting, you simply weren't whole anymore, were only half of what you were supposed to be.

Uncle Donny honks, but my laptop is still turned on and the electric blanket is still plugged in, and by the time I get everything shut off and am putting my coat on, he's at the door, not bothering to knock or ring the doorbell, going straight for the door handle. Which is locked. Which causes him to pound on the door with his fist and yell, "It's me, let me in." Which I do.

"It's the middle of the day, what are you doing locking your door for?"

Every time I came home from university for a visit, Uncle Donny would remind me over another of my mother's epic Sunday dinners, "You know, if you lived in Chatham, you could eat like this all the time." I made the mistake only once of attempting to explain to him that St. Clair College, Chatham's local academy of higher learning, was renowned more for its certificate in air conditioning repair than for its liberal arts course selection. "Which reminds me," he said, turning to my dad. "I'm gettin' water running all down the back of my damn a/c unit. Seems to me like it's working way too hard for what it's putting out." My dad poured some more creamed corn over his mashed potatoes and promised to drop by the next day and have a look. Uncle Donny never needed an air-conditioning repair man; Uncle Donny had my dad.

I get my other arm through the other coat sleeve and slap my jean pocket to make sure I've got my keys. "Do you want a pop?" I say. Uncle Donny quit drinking alcohol and began drinking pop before I was born, replacing a vodka bottle with a pop can virtually overnight, sacrificing only his teeth and giving himself a mild case of diabetes in return for the salvation of his liver and his life. Never seeing Uncle Donny drunk is one of the things I've always been most grateful for.

"What have you got?"

"Mountain Dew."

Uncle Donny makes a face.

"I've also got Diet Mountain Dew."

Uncle Donny keeps making a face; adds a dismissive shake of the head to the mix. "I've got one going in the car, let's just get a move on."

Uncle Donny doesn't approve of my not driving, not driving being a fault of mine as a man, not owning a car being a fault of mine as the grandson and son and nephew of two generations of auto workers. I was a teenage driver, of course, borrowing the family's '67 Buick Skylark every chance I got, but who needs a car in Toronto when you're nineteen, twenty-one, twenty-five? And by the time there was a reason to get behind the wheel again—car-rented road trips with Sara when we were first going out, visits to her parents or mine once we were married—Sara always did the driving because she was the better driver, and one year it just seemed silly to pay eighty bucks to renew a piece of paper that was only going to rot in my wallet. And I still don't need a driver's licence to live in Toronto. Living in Chatham, however, I'm not so independent. Living in Chatham, I need Uncle Donny.

Before he turns the key in the ignition Uncle Donny goes right for the cooler resting on the backseat, plucking out a fresh can of Cott Cola, not wanting to risk getting caught mid-destination without a fistful of his favourite beverage. I know the routine and do my passenger-side part: pop open the glove compartment and hand him the can opener; wait for him to make an equal-sized, triangle-shaped hole at each end; carefully re-wrap the dish towel around the opener before putting it back inside so it doesn't rattle around. Do they even still make Cott Cola? They definitely don't manufacture cans without push-tabs anymore. I don't ask Uncle Donny where he gets his contraband cola supply for fear he might actually tell me.

He swallows what's left in the old can before dropping it to the floor in the back, grabs the cold reinforcement from between his legs. "You given any thought as to how you're going to get everything you're keeping back to Toronto?"

"It's not going to be much."

"Well, they're not going to let you take it all on the train, I know that."

He doesn't know any such thing—Uncle Donny has never been anywhere further away than London General Hospital (for a skin cancer scare in the 1980s) and he certainly didn't take the train (riding the train when you can drive akin to an able-bodied man choosing to sit down to pee)—but I let it slide, concentrate instead on an obviously drunk man in an overcoat and fedora swaying on the girl from the park's front step, unsuccessfully fitting the key in his hand into the keyhole in the door. I hope it's not some stranger, I hope it's someone she knows. The key falls from the man's hand and he slowly descends to his knees like a very devoted something or other; jabs his hand in and out of the bush as if every time he pulls it back empty, he can't quite believe it. I hope it's not someone she knows, I hope it's some stranger.

"And isn't it about time you got hold of a real estate agent? The economy down here isn't the best these days, so you want to get on that."

It's not just that what he says makes no economic sense—nobody's working, so nobody's buying, so there's really no hurry—I also don't like being told what to do with my dying father's house, particularly because he's just that: dying, not dead. I know he's never going to get better—never going to be even *him* again—but planting a For Sale sign in the middle of the front yard of his home is a white flag I'm not comfortable flying quite yet. Besides, there have to be more things I want to hold on to that I need to pack up. At least more than half a box's worth.

"It'll happen—sooner or later," I say, pleased to take the patronizing adult role for a change.

"Well, it should be sooner than later."

"It'll happen when it happens. I've got enough on my plate at the moment."

And that, apparently, is that—until Uncle Donny rests his can in the beverage holder and pulls an envelope out of his coat pocket and hands it to me.

"What's this?"

Pause. "We might have a situation on our hands."

"What kind of situation?"

Pause. "You better read it."

Uncle Donny drives, I read. It's a good thing for him he's driving: if I was to kill him, it might mean I'd die as well in the resultant crash. Which, at the moment, does have its appeal.

"How could you let this happen?" I say.

"It's some kind of mistake."

"It had better be some kind of mistake. But how could you let it get to this? It says here you've known about it for months now."

Uncle Donny's got his can of Cott Cola back; takes a drink, then another, like if he just keeps drinking, he'll never have to answer me. "I thought it was under control."

"It says we owe Thames View over fifteen thousand dollars."

"I know."

"How is that having it under control?"

"That place isn't cheap, you know. It's the best long-care unit in town."

"What has that got to do with anything? All that matters right now is that it's the best long-care unit in town that's going to put my father out on the street unless they get the fifteen thousand dollars they say we owe them."

We sit at a red light, which gives me time to think and Uncle Donny time to apologize. Hypothetically, anyway.

"I didn't ask for this job, you know," he says. "I've got my own problems too."

"What *job*? Since when is looking after your sick brother a *job*?"

"That's not what I mean. You know that." The car is moving again, just like our tongues.

"When my dad was alive…" Uncle Donny looks at me. "You know what I mean. Before—before he was sick—anything that was wrong with your car or your TV or your eaves troughs was just a phone call away from being fixed. A phone call to my dad."

"I did plenty of things for him too, you know. It wasn't a one-way street. I helped him out all the time too."

"Letting him know when Bic razors are on sale and when Loblaws is putting their day-old donuts out isn't quite the same thing."

And now we're here, at Thames View for our afternoon visit, Dad's loving brother and devoted son united in their single-minded desire to instill warmth and cheer into yet another otherwise empty day. There's a van parked out front that's blocking our access to the free family parking spots. DENTURES ON WHEELS, it says on the side. I can't help but hope they're not here for Dad, that his teeth aren't half as decayed as his mind. Apparently, he'd be lucky if we could afford a spool of dental floss.

"You're his son." Uncle Donny says it not like he's trying to score a point, but as if he's actually reminding me of something I might have forgotten.

"So?"

"So…where were you?"

Uncle Donny has lit a cigarette while we've been waiting for the van to move; smokes it with his face almost pressed to the rolled-up window. There's smoke all around the back of his head.

"We can go now," I say.

"What?"

"The van. It's gone. We can park now."

54

Chapter Four

I COMMISERATED WITH MY DAD when he was diagnosed. I met with every new doctor every sad step of the way. From the beginning until it didn't matter anymore, we talked on the telephone two, three times a week; about the Red Wings and his yard work mostly, the other thing—the main thing—not something there was much to talk about. I was there to watch the light go out in my father's eyes.

But I could have been better. I could have done more. Of course, if I was looking for reasons to feel less guilty about things like Uncle Donny dropping the ball and me not being there to immediately recover the fumble, convincing arguments could be offered, rationalizations could be made, legitimate excuses do exist.

My wife had been alive one morning and was dead by dinner time that same day and this does tend to make one a little self-absorbed. My father's Alzheimer's was the aftershock, after the buildings had all been leveled to smoking debris and the power grid had already gone down. It was during this period that once, on the subway, nauseated by the cheesy smell of some homeless person I couldn't detect and move away from, I eventually realized it was me—I was the one who hadn't showered in days and who was probably making everyone around me queasy. When you're getting your fruit in pie form and your only exercise is walking from the couch to the fridge for more Colt 45, and Jagermeister-induced diarrhea is your idea of an effective weight-control technique, it's tough to be a flawlessly conscientious son, let alone happy.

Bottom line, though, I was, am, and will continue to be a selfish sonofabitch. And I'm okay with that. In fact, for the particular line of work I'm in, being a selfish sonofabitch is a professional prerequisite. Underpinning a poet's love of language and a playwright's ear for dialogue and a philosopher's itch for absolutes is the novelist's screaming only-child egoism that will not allow anything or anyone to stop him from doing what he wants to do: namely, playing God with the people and places he creates. And fortunate is the creator of extended works of imaginative prose whose life companion feels the very same way, whose definition of spending quality time together as a couple is, first and foremost, doing a good day's worth of what she herself cares about most, and then—and only then—killing a bottle of red wine while watching a DVD that can even be bad because two satisfied and spent people slouching on the couch at the end of the day is the only possible way of making a good day even better.

But fifteen thousand dollars by the end of the month or else.

Playing God is the easy part; it's getting along with all the other mortals that's difficult. Especially when there's no one around to drink wine and watch bad DVDs with at the end of the day.

* * *

CLICHÉS ARE SINS, AND TONIGHT, anyway, I'm an ever-lasting malefactor. Four straight hours head down at the dining room table and all I've got to show for it is words, 1,021 words. No pictures, though. No smells, either. And, most damning of all, no sounds. And how can you possibly make Ronnie Lane live on the page if you can't compel the reader to hear the music he made? I turn over the CD case with his picture on it—a half-in-the bag, naughty little woodchuck in filthy white overalls with a sparkling secret in his dancing brown eyes he somehow managed to smuggle into every one of his songs—and decide to give it another shot tomorrow night. Because if I can't look him in the eye, I sure as hell can't conjure up his soul. Maybe Monday, after I talk to the people at the bank and get Dad's financial situation sorted out, I'll have a clearer head. Right now, I need the opposite of that; right now, I need to get stoned. I tuck a bottle of red wine underneath my arm for intoxication insurance.

I've got one foot on my front step just as the girl from across the street is stepping onto hers. There's nothing she can do now except charge or retreat. She holds onto the screen door so that it doesn't slam shut and then heads right for her swing. I take my spot on the bench.

I light up and lean over, partly to help shield the joint from the stinging wind, partly to help stay warm. Of course, I don't have to be a martyr to the February cold—I am, after all, blessed with a heating blanket and a lengthy extension cord and four well-insulated walls to bump into—but I stay hunkered over where I am. The girl is behind me, but I can only presume she's doing the same.

The girl is a good teacher, I'll give her that; two tokes in and tonight's forecast looks promising: plenty of brain fog with isolated patches of pleasant confusion mixed with persistent forgetfulness. I've changed my mind; weed's a good drug after all. Good for doing nothing and wanting nothing and being nothing, but as I've got nothing in particular to do or want or be right now, I say it's good, I say it's all right.

"What? What's all right?"

Apparently, involuntary speech is one of marijuana's less appealing attributes.

"No, I—It's a nice night, I said."

"No it's not. It sucks."

Kids these days. I will *not* let this girl kill my buzz. "So why are you out here then?"

"My dad's funny that way, you know? He's not really down with the whole getting-high-in-the-house thing. What's your excuse?"

A good question. A good reason to take another toke and change the topic. "I saw someone yesterday." We both wait for what's next. I lift my head in the hope that the icy wind will help clear my head enough to finish my thought. "On your front step. He looked … suspicious."

"Fedora? White overcoat? Moustache?"

"You know him?"

"Not really."

"Not really?"

"It was my dad."

"Oh."

"Yeah. Oh."

The girl deserves to have the last word, even if it's only *Oh.* Sara and I had an understanding when it came to each other's relatives: I'm allowed to criticize my family; you're not. You're permitted—expected, even—to commiserate with my complaints; only not too enthusiastically. But it's not acceptable for you to pile on with your own objections.

This wasn't an arrangement arrived at without a certain amount of antecedent loud trial and error.

"What's on the playlist tonight?" I say. I hadn't noticed whether or not she has her iPod with her, but odds are yes. No one under the age of twenty-five, it seems, dares go anywhere anymore without being armed with either a cell phone or an iPod or an iPad or, more often than not, some combination of the three. When I was a kid, we all dreamed of one day growing up to be just like Captain Kirk and Mr. Spock, happily weighed down at the hip by all of our phasers and communicators and everything else needed to kill the bad guys and keep us in close contact with the good ones. Three decades later, I don't even wear a watch, three keys hanging from a plastic Siemens' keychain that my dad gave me my only adult concession. Thankfully, dreams don't always come true.

"I thought you didn't like music," she says.

"I never said that."

"Oh, right. It's just music made in the last twenty years you don't like."

"That's not true." And it's not—it's more like the last thirty years, roughly around the time of the fourth Ramones album—but I resent the insinuation of incipient old-fogeyism anyway. Even dinosaurs have feelings.

"Really," she says. "Who died tonight then?"

I don't ask her to repeat herself; turn around on the bench instead to better determine whether she really said what I think she just did.

"In the book you said you're writing. The one that's not a novel. Isn't that the deal? That some ex-roadie or somebody else like that that you made up talks about a bunch of different musicians that he somehow just happened to be there with when they kicked off?"

I swivel back around and decide not to tell her the topic of tonight's disquisition, and not just because it's a dinosaur's right to graze wherever he pleases. Talking about a book in progress sucks away its oxygen, fills up with contaminating chit-chat the brain-breathing empty spaces it requires to flow and sow and grow. Sometimes Sara would casually ask me what I thought about this or that subject, and I'd excitedly answer that I was writing about that very thing in the book I was working on, so for now could only say it was an interesting question I hoped to do justice to in my novel and that maybe we could talk about it after she'd had a chance to read what I had to say. To which she would usually reply that she'd really just prefer to have a conversation with her husband and not have to wait for publication day. To which I would usually get us talking about something else. Good manners get in the way of good art.

"No one you'd know," I say. "No one you'd find interesting."

"No doubt. But who is it anyway?"

"Someone who's been dead for a long time." Only about fifteen years, actually, but to an eighteen-year-old, that is a long time.

"Jim Morrison," she says.

"No."

"Jimi Hendrix," she says.

"No."

"John Lennon."

"No," I say, both to shut her up and to prove that I'm not the classic-rock zombie she obviously thinks I am. "And not Keith Moon or John Bonham or Brian Jones either."

"So who then?"

Christ, it's no wonder her old man is a drunk. "Ronnie Lane," I say.

"Is he the one from the Rolling Stones?"

I pause, and not just to take another toke, either.

"No. That's Ronnie Wood."

"What's the difference?"

"Don't you have any homework or a science project or some extracurricular activity to attend to?"

"Nope. And all my chores are done for the day, too, pa. Please tell me all about the life and times of Ronnie Lane."

If I wasn't starting to feel the effect of the weed and the house wasn't so empty and everything wasn't so not enough or too much, I'd just stand up and go. I stay where I am.

"Ronnie Lane..." I begin. "Ronnie Lane, he..." I continue.

When you can hear yourself talking, you're not really communicating. Pot may be the ideal fuel for contentedly puttering around in your own consciousness, but booze, it seems, is still the drug of choice when tongues need to be loosened and the race for the right word is preferable to slouching on the sidelines. I extinguish the joint and twist the cap off the wine bottle and take a long pull.

"I guess you're not shooting for the bestseller list with this one, are you?" the girl says.

"Give me a minute." That minute plus one more and two more slugs of wine later, I'm ready.

"Ronnie Lane was in a British band in the 1960s called the Small Faces and in another band in the '70s called the Faces. They both played rock and roll and they both played it the way it's supposed to be played: loud, rude, and horny. Around the time of the Faces' second album, though, Ronnie woke up to wooden music—US dusty high-lonesome twang goosed just right with blood-pudding British dancehall stomp—and even though the Faces' audience was getting bigger and everyone's bank account was getting fatter, Ronnie took his bass and went home, used the money he'd saved up not buying Cadillacs and rhinestone jumpsuits and vacation homes in Bermuda to purchase a farm on the English/Welsh border to raise his family on and to make his new music at, and a mobile recording studio to rent out to other bands to help pay the bills. Because the guy was no dim dreamer—it was 1973, he knew what he heard in his head wasn't what the kids watching Top of the Pops wanted to hear. He knew what he was up against. For Christsake, he called his band Slim Chance."

Offering a writer an audience is like inviting a drunk to an open bar; they simply can't help themselves. All I lack is a big blast of dexy and this freezing winter night amended to summery mild. I settle for a big swallow of red wine instead.

"But the deck wasn't stacked against him quite enough, not yet. To promote his first album with Slim Chance, he decided he wasn't going to gig the usual big city concert halls, but to bring something he called The Passing Show to every provincial outpost in England that would have failed a cost/benefit touring analysis, a rock and roll circus with clowns and jugglers and fire-eaters and, most of all, the rocket fuel mandolin music he wanted to tell everyone about. And naturally it was the wettest British summer in thirty years and the antique gypsy coaches he'd bought to haul around the musicians and their families and all of the equipment broke down every fifty miles and local firemen wanted to see permits and the sanitation officials wanted to know where exactly the portable toilets were going to be located and by the end of it they were pawning equipment just to buy enough diesel to get to the next show. Ronnie lost a small fortune and nobody bought the album, but the seventeen people who saw the show or heard the songs never purchased another Rod Stewart LP again."

The wind, a barking dog, the frozen moon. And that's just about right.

"You talk really fast for someone who smokes pot."

I hold up the wine bottle. "I had some help," I say. "I'll try to be more mellow in the future."

"Don't. Don't be more mellow."

"You don't like mellow?"

The girl doesn't answer. The barking dog does. "I hate mellow," she says.

"It has occurred to you that you might be fond of the wrong drug, then, has it not?"

The girl doesn't answer; instead, asks: "Then what?"

The sweetest sound a storyteller can hear, the two words that can defeat even a busted microphone and being clean and sober.

"Then you can imagine then what. Then there were three more records that a year after they came out you could buy in a discount bin for a buck, but now go for close to a hundred dollars each on eBay. Then he found out he had Multiple Sclerosis—MS! The guy's nickname was Plonk, he drank so much, and what does he die of but MS!—and he decided to circle his broken-down wagons and raise chickens and sheep until the coldest British winter in thirty years and the diseases that blew in with it killed most of his animals and he was forced to sell his farm and move back to London and do the best he could do trying not to hurt too much."

My hands are cold and my mouth is dry in spite of the half bottle of wine in my stomach, and I must have said something right because even I'm sad. I get up from the bench without looking at the girl and head home.

From the direction of the swing set, "What else about Ronnie Lane?"

"There is nothing else." I don't like the way that sounds. I pause at the front door. "Listen to him," I say. "Listen to Ronnie Lane."

* * *

WHEN I WOKE UP THE NEXT MORNING I felt ashamed of myself. You simply don't talk about your work. It's bad manners, it's bad for the writing itself, it's bad to blather to strangers. Bad, bad, bad.

That wasn't me, I'm not like that.

I'd rant and rave to Sara, sure. Wouldn't discuss or dissect or delineate, but when something work-related was cooking in my head, I'd occasionally spout verbal steam while we were out walking the dog together or while doing the dishes or over breakfast's second cup of tea. Which would never detract or impair what I was up to—would only, in fact, turn up the inspirational heat a notch or two higher. Someone to talk at, basically, someone to help you discover what it is you really want to say.

But that wasn't someone. That was different. That was Sara.

* * *

THERE'S A MESSAGE ON MY CELL phone from Thames View asking me to please drop by the director's office as soon as it's convenient—it's urgent—obviously the oral follow-up to the written-word warning that Uncle Donny has just sprung on me. I feel like I'm being called into the principal's office for something I didn't do but that I know I'm going to take the heat for anyway. That's what I get for forgetting for fifteen minutes what I was supposed to be so upset about. Bad news is always just one voicemail message away. I'll call them back once I'm finished at Uncle Donny's.

Visiting Uncle Donny is like seeing the Grand Canyon again for the first time in decades: the only thing that's changed is you. Maneuvering around the stacked cases of Cott Cola on the way from the cold room to the kitchen is a challenge, particularly as there's a light switch but no light bulb, Uncle Donny a firm believer that feeling your way along a wall is a cheap and effective substitute for seeing where you're going. The same gold-speckled, white Formica kitchen table supports the same two-slice toaster, dual AM radio/alarm clock, clear plastic seven-day pill dispenser, and several years' worth of *Farmer's Almanac* that were there the very first time Dad took me along on one of his innumerable service calls disguised as Uncle Donny social calls. From the wiring inside the walls to the carpeting in the hallway to the shingles on the roof, Uncle Donny's house is a museum of Dad's dedicated handiwork. For that, anyway, I'm glad I'm here, despite the reason I'm here.

I hang my coat on the back of a kitchen chair and am on my way to the living room when Uncle Donny practically steps in front of me. "That room's a mess," he says. "Let's sit in here."

The table in Uncle Donny's kitchen is for a lot of things, but eating at it, never mind simply sitting at it, has never been one of them. Just as Uncle Donny will never stand if he can sit, slouching is always preferable to sitting upright. Uncle Donny's default position is leaning back as far as his recliner will allow with the TV remote control in one hand and a cigarette and a can of Cott Cola alternating in the other.

"Like I care if it's messy," I say. Maybe it's because I'm already weary of what we're doing before we've even begun, but I'd much rather go through Dad's financial records on the couch. Or maybe it's just laziness by osmosis, a classic case of when in Uncle Donny's house, do as Uncle Donny.

"Well maybe I do," he says. "Ever since this business with your dad has been going on, I've had to let a lot of things slide around here."

"I'm sorry that your dusting time has been compromised by my dad losing his mind."

"Now, don't say that."

I can see the spark that this fight could easily flame into if I don't stamp it out. It's for times like these that I stopped taking speed. I wish I could tell someone how happy I am with the decision I made. I wish I could tell Sara.

"Look," I say. "I'm just worked up about this screw-up with Thames View. But I'm sure that once we get Dad's papers sorted out we can get to the bottom of why they think we owe them so much money."

Uncle Donny lowers his eyes and nods—once—as close to an apology as I'm going to get.

"The table will be better for what we're doing anyway," I say. "That way we can spread out all of Dad's documents so we can have a clearer idea of what we're doing."

Uncle Donny grants me another silent nod, which I reward with making the first move, pulling out the chair that my coat is draped over and sitting down. Uncle Donny goes to the cold room and comes back with two cans of Cott Cola with all of the enthusiasm of a condemned man helping himself to his last liquid meal. There's a can opener lying on the table, right next to a pink plastic back scratcher and the glass novelty bird who's been dipping his beak in and out of the same glass of water for the last thirty years, Sisyphus à la Uncle Donny. I open both cans while he goes to get the file I'd asked him to keep chronicling Dad's financial affairs since he's been at Thames View. The single-speaker cassette player that's small enough to sit on the window sill plays Frank Sinatra's greatest hits, "Summer Wind" in the middle of winter.

An hour and two cans of Cott Cola each later, we're no nearer to understanding how Thames View can be so adamant that Dad's fees are in arrears fifteen thousand dollars. Uncle Donny goes to the sink and runs the tap. Frank croons away about how he did it his way.

"I guess the thing to do is to just pay them and let it all get settled out later," he says.

Uncle Donny stands at the sink with his back to me. "Are you crazy? Why would we pay them money we don't owe them? *How* would we pay them money we don't owe them?"

Uncle Donny shuts off the tap but stays where he is, stares out the kitchen window. "I thought maybe me and you could pay them. Just until everything gets straightened out."

"Where would you and I get fifteen thousand dollars?"

He finally turns around from the sink; sticks his hand in his pants pocket and pulls out a roll of bills. "There's nearly a thousand dollars here," he says. "If you could put in the rest, maybe we could get this all behind us."

I stand up. "Uncle Donny, there's no—"

"I'd pay you back my fair share. I know I'd owe you half." He holds out the money like a begging old man with a wad of bills in his palm.

"Just put that away, okay? There's no reason for anyone to panic. I'm going to talk to someone at the bank tomorrow. That's where I probably should have gone in the first place."

"Why do you want to get the bank involved?"

"I don't want to get anyone involved. But they're probably our best bet at figuring out why Dad's cheques aren't getting through to Thames View."

Uncle Donny is looking at the money in his hand like he can't remember how it got there. "I don't know," he says, slowly shaking his head.

"You don't know what?"

Uncle Donny just shakes his head.

I take the hand with the money in it and carefully push it back inside his pants pocket. Uncle Donny isn't the sort of uncle you hug—in forty-four years, I can't remember doing it even once—but once the money is returned I rest my hand on his shoulder.

"Don't worry about it, all right? I'll take care of it. You stay home tomorrow and take a break and I'll get my own ride to Thames View. I'll bet you by this time tomorrow it'll all be sorted out. And as soon as it is, I'll give you a call, okay?"

Uncle Donny doesn't speak, but looks as if he's going to say something anyway, eyes anxious in their sockets, tongue licking his lips.

"Go get your car keys, okay?" I say. "I better get home. I've got work to get to."

Talk of my leaving returns his attention to me. "I've got a call to make," he says. "It'll only be a minute."

It's only now that I notice he's not wearing his latest and only fashion accessory. "Where's your cell phone?" I say.

"What the hell do I need a cell phone for? Do you know how much one of those things cost? It adds up, you know."

I don't argue with him, and Uncle Donny goes to his bedroom to make his phone call while I remove my coat from the back of the chair. While I'm doing up the buttons on my jacket I wander into the living room to get a peek at what Uncle Donny's idea of a mess really is.

Where I'm shocked. Not because there's stuff lying everywhere, but because there is no stuff. Almost no stuff: a crisp brown plant rotting in a green plastic pot on the floor where the TV used to be; several empty Cott Cola cans scattered around the room; a pile of Pro-Line tickets raked and ready to be made a bonfire of. But certainly none of the things that make Uncle Donny Uncle Donny, like his heated, vibrating recliner or his chair-side, glass-encased mini-fridge or his fifty-two-inch television or the revered collection of several remote controls laid out for easy access. He must have sold all of it to get the money he offered me to help pay Dad's bills. I can hear him coming down the hall, so I duck back into the kitchen.

Poor old bastard, I wouldn't want him to know that I know, I wouldn't want to embarrass him. Poor old bastard.

*　　*　　*

THE PERSON IN CHARGE OF ACCOUNTS overdue at Thames View isn't in, but everyone in room #131 has had their supper. And had their dishes cleared away and been cleaned up for the evening and had their catheters and diapers removed, emptied, and replaced. I know it's their job and they do it because they get paid to and not because this is how they'd choose to spend their weeknights if they won Lotto 6/49, but the caregivers at Thames View allow Dad and me both our dignity. I can't claim to know much that goes on inside his head, but I know Dad prefers to be clean and comfortable and well fed, and he always is. As for me, even though there's a tablespoon of guilt seasoned with a dash of shame in knowing that I couldn't possibly do for him what the strangers who work here so capably can, that's offset by the reassurance of knowing that, even if I'm not here—*especially* if I'm not here—Dad is clean and comfortable and well fed.

Speaking of dignity:

"Do you know who I am, Grandpa?"

What sounds like a man who's swallowed a chicken bone but who's too feeble—or too afraid—to do more than attempt to wheeze it free of his blocked windpipe. Between Dad's advanced Alzheimer's and the daily cocktail of drugs he takes, his days of struggling to speak, of sputtering his way to frustration, rage, and tears, are over. Not so for the man with the bed closest to the door.

"Do you know who I am, Grandpa?"

The same man, making the same terrible sound, only slightly louder and with more urgency this time, panic taking hold now, the bone clearly impeding the oxygen intended for his rapidly emptying lungs.

"He doesn't know, Donna."

"Yes he does, don't you, Grandpa? You know who I am. You know who I am, don't you? I'm Lizzy's daughter, Grandpa. I'm Donna."

The same man, the same sound, until, eventually, struggling free from somewhere, "Du, du, du…"

I can feel my own tongue and teeth involuntarily coming together to finish the man's stutter for him.

"That's it, that's it—who am I?"

"Du, du, du ... "

I can feel sweat—real sweat—pushing through the pores on my forehead while I wait for the man to complete the word, embarrassed to anxiety for both of us: for him to have to try and say it; for me to have to hear him suffer.

"You're almost there, Grandpa, you're almost there."

"Du, du, du ... "

I can feel a single drop of sweat slowly roll past my left eye and down my cheek. Obviously, for the remainder of eternity the man is doomed to never say what he wants to say, just as I'm condemned to everlastingly witness his two-syllable torture.

"Du, du, du, duna."

"Donna!" Donna shouts, clapping her hands. "That's right, I'm Donna!"

I breathe, not aware I'd been holding my breath.

"See," Donna says to her mother on the other side of her grandfather's bed. "I told you he knew who I was."

His vindicated granddaughter's identity finally established, Grandpa—actually, Mr. Goldsworthy, that's what the white plastic nameplate affixed to the end of his bed says—can now return to the incessant lip wetting and tongue sucking he seems to enjoy best. I know I'm wrong—we're all taught that until they reach Dad's irreversible silent stage the Alzheimer's patient needs to be encouraged, prodded even, back, if only temporarily, from the edge of endless night that every moment shadows his mind just a little bit more—but I can't help but be thankful that Dad's losing battle for dying daylight is over.

71

I know it's wrong, but I can't help but be relieved that Dad is past the point of putting the TV remote control in the freezer or his wristwatch in the sugar bowl, or that his mood doesn't whip from calm to tears to arms-flailing anger for no apparent reason, or that he no longer insists that one of the care workers is stealing his socks and underwear, or that he doesn't endlessly open up his wallet and take everything out only to put it all back in before five minutes later starting all over again. Where we're at—here he's at—isn't where we want to be, but since this is where we all knew we were going to end up, I'm glad that the struggle not to be here is over. I overheard one of Mr. Goldsworthy's other daughters tell the nurse that her father had been a mechanic at Chatham Motors for forty years. Any man who knew—without ever having to bother lifting the hood—every nut, bolt, and belt that made the engine run in every North American car built since about the time Diefenbaker was Prime Minster shouldn't be subjected to being tested on the name of his granddaughter. I know I'm wrong, but it's not right.

Picking up the remote and clicking on the TV, "Let's check out *NHL on the Fly*, Dad," I say. "The Wings are at home to Colorado. It's not the rivalry it used to be, but you know as well as I do that both of them still hate to lose to the other one more than to just about anybody else. This could be a good one."

Chapter Five

WAITING YOUR TURN FOR THE NEXT available customer service representative at the bank is like standing in line at customs or waiting in your car to cross the border: even if you haven't done anything wrong, it sure feels like you have. Today is Customer Appreciation Day at CIBC, but the cold coffee and warm orange juice and broken sugar cookies don't make me feel any more appreciated.

A strikingly plain, fiftyish woman, hand extended like a shark fin, is headed directly for me. I stand up before she arrives, hope she's here to welcome me and nothing else. "Mr. Samson," she says, and we shake hands.

"Would you like to come this way, then?" She directs me toward the rear of the bank, where several white cubicles without nameplates resemble a human honeycomb of bureaucracy, each worker bee invisible to the eye but clear to the ear, a steady clatter of keyboard tapping and telephone yakking accompanying us to our appointed cell at the very back. An opened palm indicates where I'm supposed to sit. I feel like a herded farm animal who's reached his final, fatal destination. I sit.

"I understand you have some questions regarding your father's account."

"The nursing home where he's at claims they haven't been receiving the monthly transfer of his expenses for quite awhile now. They get his OAS and CPP cheques directly from the government, but his pension money from the factories he worked at make up the difference of what he owes them. My Uncle Donny was supposed to make sure this was all set up. Which he did. Which it is. Which it was, I mean." I'm starting to confuse even myself. I point at the computer—this is a woman who clearly appreciates the value of the hand gesture. "Can you just tell me what's going on with his account?"

"Certainly." And with that her fingers attack the keyboard with a precise ferocity, hardly slowing down even when she glances at the manila folder open on the desk. I make books for a living yet type with two fingers. If I had her job, I wouldn't make it past lunch time of my first day. A good novel is full of all sorts of people convincingly doing all of the things that people do, but it only takes a ten-minute stroll outside your study to be reminded how utterly useless a writer is at anything except explaining the world to itself. Writers are practically Masonic in their insistence upon the difficulty of the writing life, but all except the most arrogantly entitled know that we're the ones who got off easy. Those who can, do; those who can't, and are lucky enough, write down what everyone else is doing.

The woman looks up from the screen. "Everything would seem to be fine with your father's account. It's active and up to date."

"Okay. Then why isn't his nursing home getting their money?"

"Give me another moment, please." Her fingers fly at the keyboard once again and she takes her moment and maybe one more, before, "The cheques from the various factories you spoke of were directly deposited into your father's account at one time, but at the request of your father's legal overseer, they're now mailed to your father directly at his current address, specifically"—The woman consults her file—"Thames View Gardens."

"Hold on—my father's what?"

This time the woman illustrates she's equally adept at flipping pages as she is at clacking keys. "It seems that your father's brother, a Mr. Donald Gordon Samson—I assume this is the Uncle Donny you spoke of earlier?" I nod. "Was given power of attorney by your father over his affairs before your father became a resident of Thames View Gardens."

"Okay. Right. And?" I didn't know Dad gave him power of attorney—I barely know what power of attorney is—but since Uncle Donny was handling the majority of what went on when I wasn't here, it makes sense. I guess.

"I'm not sure what else you'd like me to tell you."

"How about why my father is being threatened with eviction from his nursing home?"

"I'm sure I have no idea. That would come under your uncle's province as legally appointed overseer of your father's affairs."

It sounds so simple coming from her mouth—right up until it leaves my ears and enters my brain, when it makes absolutely no sense. "But my dad's cheques—there's more than enough there to cover his room and board and everything else he needs at Thames View."

I can see that the woman is consciously pausing before saying what she next has to say. This, I can tell, will not be the pause that refreshes.

"Did your father ever discuss with you the rights and responsibilities that come with someone having power of attorney over someone else's affairs?"

"I didn't even know my uncle had power of attorney until you just told me."

"I see." The woman lowers her eyes to her keyboard.

"So what are you saying? That my uncle has been cashing my father's cheques and keeping them for himself?"

"I'm sure I didn't say any such thing."

"But that's what you're saying."

"No—again, I didn't say anything of the sort. What I said was that you should perhaps speak to your uncle about your father's financial affairs."

"Oh, I plan to, believe me."

"Good."

"Yeah, good."

The woman escorts me to the front of the bank. I'd love to have a reason to be furious at either her or the bank or both, someone or something I could self-righteously scream at right here, right now, but when she stops walking and offers her hand and says, "I wish I could have been of more help," goddamnit—I think she actually means it.

* * *

By the time I find my feet in Tecumseh Park, I'm calmer, although it's not the thinking I do on the walk over that does the semi-soothing, it's the view of the winter-wrapped trees and the snow-dusted river and the walk to the park itself, exercise being the human body's built-in anxiety exhaust system.

I used to take the bus to the depot downtown and then walk through the park to CCI. John McGregor was the closest high school to home, but Chatham Collegiate Institute had the best football team. And if by grade eight it was apparent even to me that I wasn't NHL material after all, maybe football was my way to sports celebrity salvation. Because if at first you don't succeed, try, try again—even though everybody knows you're probably going to fail anyway. Which I did—was a starting linebacker by grade ten, but never big or fast or nasty enough to be anything more than a good high-school player—but which I didn't, either, CCI turning out to be not only a football powerhouse but, incidentally, the city's only academically elite secondary school. Not the reason I went there, but the reason I ended up being glad that I did. Mum had very clear career goals for me—to work in the air-conditioned front office of a factory like Siemens and not down on the dirty assembly line like my dad—and education, of course, had a role to play. Just not *too* much education. Too much learning, after all, being dangerous, like too many hotdogs on your birthday; was suspicious, like too much time spent alone in your bedroom. CCI made it okay to be smart. And now, apparently, it wasn't going to be there for much longer to make it okay for anyone else.

The school parking lot is full. When I went here, only the teachers and maybe half a dozen lucky students, with rich parents, parked their Tauruses and Cordobas and Trans Ams in the gravel lot. Which is a paved lot now, and where there's a shiny new black BMW parked near the school's east-side door that seems familiar, although that doesn't make any sense. Until its owner sees me staring at her car.

"I use The Club. You'd never get away with it." Rachel Turnbal has her car keys in one hand and an empty white coffee mug dangling from a pair of ring-less fingers in the other, a bulging bag—not a purse—hanging over her shoulder.

"I was … I was walking and I ended up here." Which isn't as pathetic as it sounds. Probably.

"Uh huh." Rachel unlocks the driver side door and gets in, immediately starts the car. The passenger-side window slides down just enough for me to hear, "Now that you're here, are you staying or are you going?"

I get in.

"You don't teach *here*, do you?"

"Public school. Four, five, and six." We blast out of the parking lot and I wait for the sound of spitting gravel that never arrives. "Would it be so surprising if I did?"

"No." Yes. Rachel was a CCI anomaly—offspring of parents with money who was neither beautiful nor brainy. Until now, apparently.

"Where to today?"

"Home, I suppose."

"You mean your parents' house?"

"Right. My parents' house."

The surrounding houses and the Chatham Cultural Centre and the lone variety store where we used to shoplift during lunch period: nothing has changed. Unlike at home—real home, Toronto—where sometimes you'll be in a part of the city you haven't visited for only a few months and an entire building will have vanished, the steel skeleton of another one already spearing the sky.

"And that would be where, exactly?"

"Pardon?"

"Where do you want me to take you—where exactly do your parents live?"

"Right. Sorry." Particularly when drunk-slumped in the backseat of a cab, everyone is secretly disappointed that the driver needs directions. How pleasant to believe that it's someone else's job for a change to know where you're supposed to be going.

"Do you know where Tecumseh High School was? It's a new subdivision near there."

"Buttercup Village?" Rachel registers my surprise. "I teach at Tecumseh Public School."

"Is that what the high school is now?" Rachel spares me a nod while concentrating on executing a perilous pass of an idling garbage truck.

"I don't know why," I say, "but I thought it was a day-care centre."

"Don't feel bad," Rachel says, garbage truck behind us and the Beemer back up to speed. "Sometimes that's what it feels like to me too. And I work there."

Rachel always was witty. Back in high school, though, I was too young to know that the funnier a person is, the more intelligent they're likely to be. Novels, human beings, films: it's easy to forget that *cosmic* is just *comic* with a single extra letter. Fêted appearances to the phony contrary, a solemn book is a shallow book. Ditto pompous people and pretentious movies. Tragedy without comedy is like a brain without a heart.

"So you must have been leaving school the time before, when you picked me up last time."

"What's wrong? Don't you believe in fate?"

Instead of squirming, I smile, a squirmy smile; Rachel laughs.

"Don't worry," she says. "I don't either." And just to emphasize her point—either that, or to contradict it—she pats my thigh a couple of quick times.

Both hands back on the steering wheel, "I heard about your wife," Rachel says. "I can't imagine what that must have felt like. What it feels like."

I look out the window. Duplex after duplex so similar in size, shape, and colour, if there weren't black metal numbers hanging over the front doors, their occupants likely wouldn't be able to tell which one was theirs. "Thanks," I say.

"For what?"

"For not saying you're sorry."

Everyone says they're sorry—sorry to hear it, sorry for your loss, sorry for you. The griever can't use *sorry*. And to say that you're sorry says that you know what their hurt feels like, thereby making that hurt seem just a little a bit less theirs. The only thing the griever gets in return for his pain is the privilege of it being his pain and no one else's. It hurts—it burns—but it's his.

Rachel doesn't reply—the perfect reply—and we're turning in at the gates of Buttercup Village. I feel like if I just sit here, just let her keep driving, she'll pull right up into my parents' driveway without another word from me. Because I don't want to find out I'm wrong, "It's right here, near the little park at the end, number two."

Buttercup Village wasn't built for high-powered automobiles operated by exceptionally self-assured drivers with an inclination toward going much, much too fast, and I like the idea of every set of curtains and blinds along Dahlia Avenue blowing in the reverberating breeze in spite of every frozen-shut window, every irate home owner punching in the last desperate digit of 911.

"Okay, good to see you—again—and take care of yourself, okay?" No awkward goodbye, no pretend promise to stay in touch, no final farewell pat on the thigh. Excellent. Just the way I want it: easy and honest. Excellent. Not even one friendly tap. Not one.

I'm on the front step when I turn around at the roar coming down the street—Rachel, in reverse, travelling just as fast backward as when she left.

"There's a meeting tomorrow night at CCI about the closing. It's going to be pretty important. From seven until about nine. Some of us usually go for a drink afterward. You should come."

And then she's gone again.

* * *

I CALL UNCLE DONNY WITHOUT telling him what I know and decide to wait for him on the front porch. In part, because I don't want to waste any time interrogating him; in part, because the freezing breeze might help cool off my baking brain. Just then a fat man in a white snowsuit and black wrap-around sunglasses too small for his flabby, wind-burnt face zips by the house, on a tiny, child-sized motorbike, the screech of the bike's buzz saw motor polluting the air almost as much as the clouds of smoke trailing behind. He looks like a circus midget who's lost his costume and make-up privileges and turned to steroids and corndogs in consolation. I almost don't believe he was there until, once around the block, he passes me again, joylessly staring straight ahead down the empty street.

"Spring can't be far off now. The goggly-eyed, two-wheeled thunder bum has made his glorious return."

The girl from the park, in the park—I hadn't noticed. Probably because it's the first time I've seen her in the daylight. "School holiday?" I call from my porch.

"I'm taking a mental health day."

The phone and iPod are laid out beside her on the bench, an unlit joint between her lips. "I can see that," I say.

"You know what they say: 'Physician, heal thyself.'"

"Right."

Its apparent uselessness to me as a conversation starter and sustainer aside, weed is no different from any other drug, whether it's the government-taxed, over-the-counter variety or the kind you can only get from a guy named Bubba who lives in his mother's basement: booze or drugs or any combination thereof are for when the day is done, the shade of a cooling consciousness best enjoyed only after first overheating one's head in the busy glare of the day. Shade without light is invisible, isn't anything. Beware of not anything. But what the hell, I've got enough problems keeping my own train on the track. Choo choo to you, then, my teenage friend, and here's hoping you eventually make it to the station safe and on time and with the majority of your brain cells intact.

The fat man on the mini-bike chugs past us again, his knees nearly at his chin; it takes a moment for one's ears to adjust to the after-assault quiet. Once they do, "So was that your wife or something?" the girl says.

"My wife?"

"The BMW that dropped you off. Was that her driving?" The joint is out of her mouth now and in her hand, still unlit.

"No, that was"—yes, that was what, exactly?—"a friend," I decide. Deciding even that somehow sounds salacious, "She's involved in the campaign to keep CCI open. You should be thankful that people like her are working so hard to help keep your school from closing."

"It's not my school."

"You go there, don't you?"

"For, like, five more months."

"Well, without people like her there won't be many more months for anyone."

"Whatever." The girl picks up her phone and looks at it as if she's expecting it to ring. It doesn't. "Does your wife know about your friend? Your wife—she's back in Toronto, right?"

"My wife is dead," I say.

The girl looks up from her phone. "Oh."

I don't say anything else, let her smutty smear hang in the air between us like a bad smell no one wants to own up to. She puts down the phone and lights up the joint.

"I'm sorry," she says.

Here we go again, that word, that same worthless word. "Don't be. It wasn't your car that killed her."

"I mean I'm sorry for implying that you ... you know. I mean, I saw your wedding ring, so I just ... " The girl stubs out the just-lit joint on the bench with a quick, single stab and grabs her phone and iPod. She keeps her eyes on her running shoes all the way across the park.

"My name's Sam," I say.

The girl slows down, but doesn't stop her retreat home. By the time she gets to the street, though, the fat man is blasting past again, keeping her on the curb. She waves away a swirl of black exhaust but can't help coughing, a half-and-half mix of hacking and laughing eventually taking its place. I can't help laughing too.

"Samantha," the girl manages, again without looking my way.

"Hello, Samantha," I say.

"Hello, Sam."

*　*　*

NO ONE VISITING ROOM #131 is self-conscious about talking to themselves. That's one of the best things about dad sharing a room with three other residents. At first, I was opposed—nothing too good for my father, only the priciest private room will do—but once we actually got him moved into Thames View I was reminded once again how what is normal and nice is what is happening to you right now. We *all* talk to ourselves in room #131. We *all* pretend to varying degrees that our loved one is listening and is interested and is happy that we're here. Make believe is so much easier when everyone else is doing it too. Alzheimer's is lonely enough; a silent, solitary room isn't what the Alzheimer sufferer needs. Isn't what his family needs, either.

And so what if it isn't true? I didn't say it was true—I said it was nice. And everyone in room #131 can use all of the nice they can get. *I* can use all of the nice I can get. Particularly after the conversation I finally had with Uncle Donny.

"You thought that the government would pay for it."

"I told you, just until I could win back what I lost."

"Win back fifteen thousand dollars. Which means that you lost fifteen thousand dollars."

"Give or take."

"Give or take? You're a seventy-four year old retired factory worker from International Harvester on a fixed income and all of a sudden it's 'fifteen thousand dollars, give or take.' Since when did you become the Cincinnati Kid? "

"I don't know how it happened. I really don't. After I retired, I guess I had more time on my hands than I knew what to do with. And at first it wasn't that much—just Pro-Line mostly, usually no more than fifty bucks a week, a hundred at most—but then it got out of hand. I guess I got in over my head."

"Believe me, you were in over your head before you placed your first bet. *Way* over."

"You've got to understand, I didn't mean to get anyone else involved in this. I thought that the government would help us out until I could get back what I lost."

"You thought that until you won back fifteen thousand dollars in gambling debts the government was going to step in and pay Dad's bills."

"Now you're not even listening, now you're just repeating what I'm saying."

"No, I'm just trying to understand how you could be so goddamn stupid."

"A man works as hard as your father did his whole life, paying into the system his whole life, you'd think there might be a little something somewhere to help a guy out when he needs a helping hand."

"There is. They're called pensions. You know: those things of his that you stole."

"You keep calling it that doesn't make it true, you know."

"What would you call signing his cheques and cashing them in and pissing them away on gambling debts?"

"Not just that. Not just that. I got my roof fixed too."

"Sorry, my mistake. Gambling debts and home renovations."

"So now you're saying I don't deserve to have a roof over my head that doesn't leak."

"This isn't about you. That's the part of this you don't seem to understand. This is about my father."

"He's not just your dad, you know. He's my brother."

"Your brother that you robbed blind."

"That's not right, that's not right for you to say that."

"Well, don't worry, I won't be saying it again. Just like you're not going to be visiting him again."

"It's a free country. You can't stop me from visiting my own brother."

"It won't be free for you for very much longer if I tell the police what you managed to pull off. I don't want you even coming near Thames View. And if I find out that you have, you're going to be placing all future bets from behind bars."

"What I've got—it's a disease, you know."

"How is it that whenever somebody screws somebody else around it's always because they have a disease, but the entire time they were busy doing it, it was nobody else's business but their own?"

"I'm getting help with my addiction at Chatham Mental Health now. I haven't played Pro-Line or placed a bet over the phone in two days. I even got rid of my cell phone."

"Two days. Congratulations. Maybe Dad's cheques will be safe until the end of the month."

"Damn it, I told you, that's all over now."

"Well, you got that part right, anyway."

"Which part?"

"The part about it being all over."

Chapter Six

I CAN WALK FROM THE NURSING home to the bar.

The bar, the Montreal House, was here when my dad was a young man; the nursing home—under its older name and function—as well. Before the developers and their bullying bulldozers ate up the farm land and shat back the shiny piles of surrounding suburbs in their place, Chatham existed for the human beings who erected it. People once-upon-a-time really did walk to the store on the corner and ran to the neighbourhood baseball field and meandered to the school just on the other side of the bridge. I walk across the ice-glazed parking lots of a carpet wholesaler, a hot-tub installer, and a lube and oil-change garage, careful not to step onto the road, a lone pedestrian just an overgrown squirrel too goddamn stupid to own a car.

Of course, if the world ran on reason—and if sane social planning was as common as greed, stupidity, and sloth—no double-digit-an-hour-paying factory would have hired my grade-nine-dropout father to help quench the country's car lust and I would probably be—at best—a second-genera-tion custodian whose only notable life experience outside Chatham city limits would probably have been something akin to an endlessly-recalled weekend in my early-twenties spent attending Wrestlemania at the Pontiac Silverdome in Detroit in the late-eighties, that long ago golden age when the name Hulk Hogan still meant something and Bon Jovi owned the airwaves. This is called irony. Employed in literature, it is quite often illuminating, if not for the characters, then at least for the reader. Unfortunately, this is freezing night-time February in Chatham, Ontario. The implication is obvious.

Inside the Montreal House there's no sign of Steady Eddie, who I'd agreed to meet here, but it's one more Friday night and everyone is drunk and intent upon getting much, much drunker, and that's all right because it's Friday night, the lie that keeps the entire working world spinning on its bone-weary axis. Give us this day our weekly whoop-up and let us forgive ourselves for wasting our lives, as we forgive those who have wasted our lives against us. And lead us not into the drunk tank tonight, but deliver us from the evil of Monday morning, forever and ever Monday morning, all men.

"Sammy!"

Steady Eddie is the only person who calls me Sammy, and then only when he's pissed. I push my way to the rear of the bar, toward where the washroom is. The Men's washroom. The Women's is located in the other room, in what was once the ladies' section of the Montreal House, at one time thoughtfully outfitted with not only its very own restroom facilities but a separate entrance as well, bygone hallmarks of a kinder, simpler, even more ignorant age. Besides the usual work-week-done revelers, tonight the place is crowded with men's rec-league hockey teams guzzling pitchers of beer and telling bad jokes, but come springtime there'll be just as many softball-playing women doing their own post-game imbibing while repeating many of these very same ha-ha's. No one ever said progress had to be pretty.

"Get your butt over here," Eddie says, dragging a chair from a nearby table by its back legs. Once we're both settled he grabs one of the three plastic pitchers and pours a glass foamy full, pushes it in front of me.

"You know Dougie Unger and Kevin Wright and Billy Rankin, don't you?" Eddie knows everyone in Chatham—even in high-school we used to call him "The Mayor"—but the guys he works with and plays weekend hockey with aren't even names without faces for me, the days of my being friends with His Honour Steady Eddie meaning that all the world was my friend, too, long gone the same day I graduated to university, Eddie to the assembly line.

Two fresh pitchers on my credit card do what an entire evening of Toronto cocktail party chit-chat could never accomplish, propel me from stranger to brand-new-buddy status in the time it takes the first sixty ounces of soapy beer to turn into suds. I'd forgotten how easy it is to hop right on and ride the bike of Chatham barroom buffoonery.

First you laugh at someone else's tasteless joke, in this case Dougie's (or Kevin's or Billy's, it's hard to tell them apart):

"These two drunks are walking down the street when they come across this dog sitting on the curb licking his balls. After awhile one of them says, 'I sure wish I could do that!' The other guy just looks at him and says, 'Well, I think you better pet him first.'"

Next, you tell your own:

"Know what the difference between Michael Jackson and a grocery bag was? One was made of plastic and was dangerous for children to play with. The other one you used to carry groceries."

Finally, someone emits an angry blast of gas—in this case, Steady Eddie, accompanied by the happy rejoinder "Speak, o' toothless one"—which elicits not only groans of delighted disapproval from everyone present except the defiantly proud blaster, but four rapidly raised glasses and the sudden panic of three empty pitchers. It's not my round, but I can use a time out. Willful imbecility is a great place to visit, you just wouldn't want to live there.

Waiting for the girl to fill the pitchers—she can't be a girl if she's slinging beer, although the blonde ponytail tied back with a blue ribbon and the gum-snapping boredom argue otherwise—I turn toward the eruption of women's laughter from the other room. I wonder if it's Rachel and a tableful of other CCI do-gooders; wonder enough that I stroll over and peek my head around the corner to discover that it's not, is just two middle-age women in Swiss Chalet uniforms, each with a bottle of Coors Light in front of her. I pay for the pitchers and am surprised I'm disappointed it's not her.

When I return with the pitchers Steady Eddie is telling a story about his brother Todd. If Todd hadn't already been the coolest person we knew simply by virtue of being twenty-years-old when Eddie and I were only eleven, his job as a Lay's Chips delivery man clearly sealed the deal. Number one, he got to ride around all day in a truck—a truck!—and number two, what was he hauling but a thirty-foot-long cabin full of potato chips. Anytime the mood strikes you, just pull that big rig over to the side of the road, good buddy, and help yourself to whatever flavour you like. It didn't seem possible that any one person could be so lucky.

"So after conning Mum into letting him have Dad's new car so he'd be able to look for sales jobs, not a month later he ends up selling it to some other loser he knows for a thousand bucks straight up, but without the owner-ship and the tags—tells the guy not to worry, the car is his outright, and the guy believes him—so when the car gets repossessed, this other nitwit, he threatens to call the cops unless Todd gives him his grand back, plus an extra five hundred for all the inconvenience." Eddie lifts his glass, but doesn't drink, is waiting until he's delivered the *coup de grace* we all know is coming. "Which of course Mum does. When hasn't she cleaned up one of Todd's messes? Which puts her out not only fifteen hundred bucks but also a two-year-old car with less than a thousand clicks on it *plus* the nearly five grand already lost on the down pay-ment Dad made before he got sick." Now Eddie can drink. "Todd. You know what I say to Mum? I say, 'He's not my brother—he's your son.'"

I wonder what happened to Todd's potato chip truck. And his expensive stereo Eddie and I weren't allowed to touch, but we'd play anyway when Todd was at work. And the white Les Paul, on which Todd could play nothing but the introduction to "Smoke on the Water," but which looked so fantastic museumed in the corner of his bed-room on its shiny silver stand. Maybe everyone only gets so much luck in their life. Maybe Todd used all of his up.

Dougie or Kevin or Billy decides that things have got-ten just a little too grown-up, so one or another launches into another sure-fire knee-slapper. "This guy answers the phone and it's an Emergency Room doctor. The doctor says, 'Your wife was in a serious car accident and I have bad news and good news. The bad news is she's lost all use of both arms and both legs and will need help eating and going to the bathroom for the rest of her life.' The guy says, 'My God. What's the good news?' The doctor says, 'I'm just kidding. She's actually dead.'"

Everyone howls but Eddie and me. We drink until the other three raise their own glasses. Eddie puts on a wild smile and leans over like he's about to tell me the world's lewdest limerick. "They don't know, they didn't mean anything."

"No problem," I say.

"You know what's what, that's all that matters."

"It's not a problem."

Someone says, "What's not a problem?" and Eddie answers back, "Guy walks into the doctor's office and says he's got a real memory problem, he can't remember anything at all. The doctor says, 'How long have you had this problem?' Guy says, 'What problem?'"

"Hilarious."

"That's fucking hilarious."

"That *is* hilarious."

"That really is."

* * *

WHAT I WANT IS MUSIC AND WARMTH, not wintertime's squall and shiver, but ten minutes after arriving home from the Montreal House, ten minutes spent on my mother's couch listening to CDs through tiny tinny earbuds sends me outdoors with a bottle of wine and a determination to track down a record player as soon as possible. I thought I'd be busy enough taking care of Dad's affairs and working on the new book that digitized music on an old Discman would suffice until I got home. It won't. Music is magic and magic needs conjuring, otherwise it's just entertainment. Music magic means I need a record player.

Besides, my phone is inside, and on it Uncle Donny's latest message, unlistened to but unlikely to be different from the previous three. Uncle Donny was the only uncle I had who never forgot to give me a birthday present—the same five dollars tucked into my shirt pocket that seemed like such a small fortune when I was ten, but which had shrunken to a deflationary family in-joke by the time I was sixteen—and could be annually counted on for an always groan-worthy "See you next year" farewell after enjoying another of my mother's Christmas turkeys, but repeated apologies and inquiries after Dad's well-being don't make up for months of systematic embezzlement. Blood isn't thicker than the misappropriation of entrusted family funds.

I'm getting used to this bench, this park. Maybe a few frozen wooden slats and a patch of partitioned dirt are all anyone needs. Or maybe I'm just drunk. Red wine was another thing Sara taught me. Not etiquette tricks like what year and vintage to purchase or what kind of cheese to eat with it, but how a full-bodied red, even if slugged right out of the bottle, is as close as alcohol can come to a conduit of cosmic consciousness, every other bottled spirit hurling you along happily with every sip toward this and that thing but never ever The Thing. William Blake didn't need booze to glimpse a world in a grain of sand, but since most of us aren't William Blake, these hard hoary stars in the sky above me and this icy air feeding my lungs and the music I can hear in my head if not in my ears are closer to what they really are because of the 2009 Hecula Monastrell stirring in my stomach. Doctors and dieticians will tell you that alcohol is only empty calories. They're wrong. Empty is just about the only thing it's not.

All I've got is the moon and a streetlight, but it looks as if the girl—Samantha—is talking to someone in her front yard. *Looks as if,* because although they're standing face to face and both busily gesturing with their hands, I can't hear a word either one of them is saying. Young lovers' quarrel, probably: fiery whispers, bursting hearts, I'll die tonight if you don't say yes or no or something else equally epochal. I'm disappointed she's capable of such an out-and-out teenage cliché. Disappointment that is, it must be admitted, odd, considering that she is, after all, a teenager.

A car comes around the corner—rude headlights on the rain-glistened street, *unta-unta-unta* thumping dance music in danger of bursting the car's windows—and slams to a stop in front of her house. The boy she's talking to drops his hands and climbs into the backseat. The car speeds off, leaving Samantha standing alone in the middle of her yard. She looks like she's considering going back inside, but crosses the street and walks past me without returning my nod and smile volley, takes her usual sulking spot on the swing.

"Boyfriend trouble?" I say.

"He's my brother," she says, the roll of her eyes audible in her voice. "And he's fourteen."

"Oh." I need a quick recovery so as not to appear to be the hopelessly out of it fuddy-duddy I so obviously seem. "In that case, you might want to tell him he's going to go deaf listening to that shit his friends were playing. In addition to ruining his sense of taste."

"It's too late. He already is."

"Already is what?"

"Deaf."

I lift the wine bottle. Red wine isn't just an excellent means of stripping the obfuscating veil of familiarity from everyday objects and events—it also does a

94

swell job of helping you forget stuff. Like how easily an eighteen-year-old girl can make you feel like an unqualified fool.

From the swing set behind me, "Speaking of shit, that shit you're drinking will end up ruining a lot more than your sense of taste."

"You are aware, I presume, of the expression 'The pot calling the kettle black?'"

"I don't drink alcohol. I don't. And pot isn't a drug."

"I see. I wasn't aware of that."

She pauses, presumably to puff. "It's an herb. It grows naturally."

"So does Athlete's Foot. That doesn't mean you want to put it inside your body."

An SUV rolls past. The bored faces of two small children strapped into the backseat are briefly illuminated by a flashing video screen. They're talking about making smoking inside automobiles illegal when there are children aboard. If they really cared about them, they'd make televisions against the law, and not just in cars.

"Anyway," the voice to my rear says, "in case you forgot, you smoke weed too. On doctor's orders, if I recall."

"I'm starting to think that the cure is worse than the disease."

"You should listen to your doctor."

"Do you?"

I pull on my bottle, she sucks on her joint. It's started to snow.

"I'd listen to a real doctor," she says. "My doctor's not a doctor, she's a shrink."

"I'm sure she knows what she's doing. And if she's not helping you, why do you go then?"

"Duh. Do you really think it's my choice?"

Actually, no, I hadn't thought about it. "Why wouldn't it be?"

Samantha sighs. Ordinarily, only people in hauntingly lyrical novels or daytime television dramas sigh. Samantha sighed.

"Who died tonight?" she says. "In your book, I mean. What musician died that you wrote about and what important moral lesson will we all no doubt glean from it."

Sarcasm—even when directed at you—is always preferable to sadness, particularly Sara sadness, so, "Buddy Holly," I say. "Buddy Holly died tonight."

"The plane crash guy?"

"The plane crash guy."

Fine snow drifts across the road, like the snow that fell that night fifty years ago and blew across three bodies scattered across an Iowa cornfield. But the story of the rise and fall and 40,000 foot crash of Buddy Holly isn't happening tonight. Crashes of any kind are definitely not on tonight's agenda.

"And?"

"And what?"

"And what's so special about Buddy Holly?"

"You've got ears, listen for yourself." Reminded of her brother, "Your brother and you—you were signing pretty intensely."

"You won't tell me about Buddy Holly, but you know what people are saying when they're signing?"

"I know when people are intense."

I drink. The wine is cold in my mouth but warm in my stomach.

"He's a little shit," she finally says.

I consider answering, but lift the bottle again instead.

"But the little shit is my brother, which makes him twice the asshole he already is when he acts like such a ... "

"A little shit?"

"You know, if that whole writing thing doesn't work out for you, you could have quite a future in family counselling. You really do have the knack."

Undeterred, "I thought being a little shit is what younger brothers did."

"Haven't you got enough dysfunction in your own family?"

I nod before realizing she can't see me. "Point taken."

"So tell me about Buddy Holly. He's got to be more interesting than our stupid families."

"What I want to do is listen to Buddy Holly."

"What's stopping you?"

"I don't have my record player."

"You mean like what DJs use, in clubs?"

"No, not like DJs use in clubs. Like in sound. Like in superior sound."

"I thought records were supposed to skip and stuff."

"And stuff, yeah. Stuff like a vinyl record being an analog recording and CDs and MP3s and all the rest of them being digital recordings, meaning that digital recordings take snapshots of the analog signal of a musical waveform and measures each snapshot with only a certain degree of accuracy, which means that by definition a digital recording is not capturing the complete sound wave, is only approximating it. Stuff like since a record has a groove carved right into it that mirrors the original sound's waveform, no information is lost. Which means that the waveforms from a vinyl recording can be much more accurate, which can be clearly heard in the richness and warmth of the resonance."

"You mean records sound better."

"You could put it like that."

Lifting the bottle—even fanatics needs fuel—"You're right, though," I say. "There is a downside. Any specks of dust or damage to the record, like scratches, can end up as skips or pops or static. Digital recordings are like robots: they're quietly effective and they never get old. Records are like people. They get noisy. They get noisy and then they get hard to hear and then they die."

I let the back-to-back honking announcement of a locked car half a street down double dot the end of my sentence. I hadn't noticed any automobile pass by. Paying attention to what's important tends to make one blind to everything else.

"If it's so important, why didn't you bring your record player and some of your records with you then?" Samantha says.

"I guess I didn't think I was going to be here long enough for it to matter."

"I guess you were wrong."

"I guess I was."

My bottle is almost empty and her joint has to be dead. There's nothing left to do for either of us but go home.

"I've got Creature Speakers," she says.

I turn halfway around on the bench, rest an arm across its back. "That's either the beginning of a confession I don't want to hear or the first line of a joke I don't understand."

"That's what I have to hook up to my iPod. I can go home and get them and download some Buddy Holly and we can listen to him."

"At my parents' house, you mean."

"It's not as if they're coming back any time soon, are they?"

"No."

"And it's what you said you wanted to do, isn't it?"

"Yeah."

"I could be back in ten minutes, probably more like five."

"Okay."

"Okay?

"Okay."

I know I've made a mistake as soon as I stand up and have to sit right back down. A semi-drunk forty-four-year-old man plus a stoned eighteen-year-old girl plus the greatest hits of Buddy Holly can't add up to anything but something you shouldn't be doing. "Samantha," I call out.

She turns around. She's smiling. It's the first time I've ever seen her look happy.

"Don't take all night, all right?"

"Ten minutes, tops."

Inside the house there's nothing to tidy up or put away because there isn't anything. The only things that would indicate I've even been here are the abandoned Discman lying on the couch where I left it and my laptop on the kitchen table. I go into the bathroom to take a pee and splash cold water on my face, use the same towel I've been using all week to dry off. It smells how I feel: used-up and mildewy. Because I worked from home and my schedule was more flexible, I was in charge of laundry. Even Sara's dirty clothes smelt good. Mine, you'd be wise to use surgical gloves to get them from the laundry basket to the washer, but hers weren't even really dirty, just more like Sara.

The doorbell rings, the first time since I've been here. Doorbells still make me jumpy, a part of me still expecting Barney to charge the door, fangs bared and barking. Especially if you were asleep or reading, this could be disconcerting, the near-heart attack you endured not quite worth the advance warning that the mailman was delivering the gas bill. No fatal coronaries were ever suffered, however, and Barney felt needed and we felt protected and what's a little uproar among loved ones? Clamour and clatter are the inevitable byproducts of a happy home.

I answer the door and Samantha pushes past me to the living room with a Holt Renfrew bag drooping full of brand-new-to-me technology. I move out of the way like a matador who's lost his cape. I watch her set up her equipment on my mother's mahogany coffee table and I pour what's left of my wine into a milk glass. It's a good thing the dead only haunt you for things done to them when they were alive—my mother didn't allow even coffee on her coffee table, let alone an iPod and Creature Speakers. The number of new fingerprints Samantha's responsible for alone would be enough to necessitate an exorcism.

"Do you want a Mountain Dew?" I say.

Samantha is on her knees on the carpet, finishing her setup, still in her coat. She stops what she's doing and looks up, pulls off her hood while considering my question, a revelation of long brown hair released from underneath. She has chestnut brown eyes and a plump, lipstick-less mouth, and although still a little baby-fattish in the face, is just one appetite-arresting bad break-up away from being what anyone would call beautiful. "You get wine and I get Mountain Dew?"

"I thought you didn't … ?"

I pull another milk glass down from the cupboard and am pouring what there is of my wine into it when, "I don't drink," she says, and goes back to work. I transfer her wine back to my glass and wonder how much music we have to listen to before I can ask her to leave. Now that I suddenly need fifteen thousand dollars and fast, I've finally made an appointment with a real estate agent who's coming by tomorrow morning at ten, and I am way behind on my packing, and—

"We're all set," she says, popping up from the floor to the couch. I stay where I am in the kitchen.

"You can take your coat off if you want," I say.

"I'd just have to put it back on later."

"That might be the single laziest thing I've ever heard." She looks around the room. "Besides, it's freezing in here."

"It's the furnace."

"What's wrong with it?"

"It's not on."

"Of course not. It's February. Why would it be?" She touches a fingertip to the palm-sized, pinky-thick piece of white plastic propped up on the coffee table and out of it miracles the ring of Buddy Holly's white Fender Telecaster closely followed by his hollering hiccupping voice and "That'll be the Day," yes, that'll be the day—when I die. By the time "Oh Boy" begins I find myself standing in the middle of the living room, and when "Rave On" comes on, I'm three-chording rhythm air guitar accompaniment to Buddy's brush-and-broom stroke lead. If I wasn't old enough to be her father, I'd ask—no: insist—that Samantha stand up and join me and dance. Instead, I look over and see her holding a framed picture of Sara and me at our wedding.

"Turn it off," I shout.

"What?" The music's not so loud she can't hear me; as suspected, I've startled her, she wasn't listening.

Jabbing at the iPod with the forefinger of my strumming hand, "Turn it off. If you're not going to listen, just turn it off."

"I was listening."

"I said turn it off."

"Fine. Whatever." She slams the picture back down on the end table and does what I asked; looks at me; crosses her arms; glares at the iPod. The house is quiet again. I wish I could remove the air guitar still slung over my shoulder without anyone noticing.

"You didn't have to yell at me," she says.

"I didn't yell at you. I just asked you to turn the music off."

"I would have turned it off if that's what you wanted. You didn't have to yell."

"I'm telling you, I wasn't yelling." Realizing I'm probably yelling, I sit down on the coffee table across from her.

"Look, I'm sorry, all right?" I say.

She looks off into the corner of the kitchen, in the direction of my mother's miniature spoon collection hanging on the wall. The slits that were once her eyes tell me she's about to either slug me or cry. I hope it's the former. Anytime Sara would cry, she could have made me do anything. She knew it, too, so she never did.

"Look," I say, "you're right, I shouldn't have yelled. Between the wine and where I was earlier tonight and what … Anyway, that's not your problem. The point is, I shouldn't have yelled."

She wipes away her scowl with the sleeve of her jacket. I can tell she's looking at me to determine if I'm telling the truth.

"So what's the big deal with Buddy Holly?" she says.

I shake my head. "You don't give up, do you?"

She buries her hands in the pouch of her hoodie, shrugs.

"Buddy Holly died," I say.

"What's so special about that?"

"Nothing," I say. "There's nothing special about it all."

* * *

.

AT 4:11 AM IT'S NOT THE THINGS you adored about her that you remember.

It was how when she sneezed it was always three times, each sneeze separated by precisely three seconds. It was how when she was tired she'd get cranky and deny it was because she was tired, that it was me saying she was cranky that was making her that way. It was how we could watch the same movie together and yet in six months she'd suggest watching it all over again, having forgotten nearly everything about it. It was how although I was the stay-at-home one and not-just-a-little-bit proprietary-proud to be in charge of the laundry and the mopping and the dishes, when for whatever reason she took it upon herself to do any of them, she did a better job than I ever did. It was how Barney followed her around the house like a hundred pound black lab baby duck, never bothering to visit me in my downstairs office unless Sara led the way. It was how she'd only eat the tops off muffins and expect me to eat the rest and would always leave the last inch of milk in the carton for me to finish. It was how she understood Bob Dylan's music better than I do but couldn't name more than ten song titles if her life depended on it. It was how at bedtime she'd complain that I kept the thermostat too low but by morning her feet would be sticking outside the blankets. It was how if she said a tree in our front yard needed trimming—otherwise one of its branches might fall on the house—and I said she worried too much, that you couldn't spend all of your time trying to out-guess life's next move, the branch would invariably fall and hit the house. It was how she'd confuse John Cale with J.J. Cale and the Flying Burrito Brothers with the International Submarine Band and not be bothered by it in the least. It was how she wouldn't want me to use aspirin when I had a headache (bad for my liver) or how Drano was a no-go when we had a sink clog (bad for the planet) or how plastic bags weren't good enough for picking up after Barney, we needed pet store-purchased bio-degradable pooch-poo pouches (better for the planet). It was how I'd periodically resign myself to a loving but understandably lust-reduced long-term relationship and then spot her in another aisle at the grocery store or coming home along the sidewalk with Barney from their walk and have my body remind me that my brain didn't know what it was talking about.

It was how I'd find myself awake at 4:11 AM, when the only thoughts you're likely to have are thoughts you shouldn't have, and I'd anchor my hand to her hip to help me flee my mind and she'd inevitably roll over without waking up before I fell back asleep, but it would be all right, I'd know she was there, I'd know I wasn't alone.

Chapter Seven

THE NAME DIDN'T CLICK UNTIL I saw the face. Oh, *that* Laura Mackenzie. Laura Mackenzie, daughter of two-term Chatham Mayor Denis Mackenzie, the same Laura Mackenzie who was CCI's head cheerleader, grade thirteen Prom Queen, and understood to be most likely to attend university for the express purpose of marrying the right kind of up-and-coming young man able to take care of her in the style she so deserved and to give her the beautiful babies nature intended her to have. All of which occurred according to plan apparently, and if you don't believe her, just take a look at the photographs on her phone. Laura reigned near the top of the high-school hierarchy, treating her fellow-student subjects with mostly benign indifference. Encouraged by her long red finger-nails and the spiked heels visible underneath the flares of her blue pantsuit, I'm predisposed to dislike her all over again. Surprisingly, I don't, both because she conveys an unexpected familiarity with what I do for a living and because she makes no secret of her disastrous first mar-riage and her second husband Bob's ongoing heart prob-lems. It's hard not to like a person who doesn't attempt to hide their hurt.

"Sometimes, though, it does feel like work," she says, taking the other end of the measuring tape and walking to the opposite end of my parents' living room. "It's like you've got to accept it almost as a job. Otherwise you'd start feeling sorry for yourself. And Bob doesn't need that. None of us needs that. But sometimes it feels like if we're not at the hospital, we're seeing specialists in London or Toronto. Thankfully Barbara and Trevor are both in university now and doing great, just great. They're my kids from my first marriage. It's Justin and Jennifer—my two youngest, Bob's and my kids—who I worry about. They love their dad and understand what he's going through, but they're kids, you know? Okay, now you stand over there and we'll get the width. I just sold a two-bedroom, two-bath, finished basement, one-car-garage rancher just like this one over on Wyandot last month and the living room was 250 square feet."

I go to where I'm told and hold the measuring tape taut and Laura reads what's there; tells me to let go of my end and I do, watch the yellow metal tape slither back inside its silver shell. When she writes down the measurements on her clipboard, I can't help myself. "How many feet?" I say.

Laura permits herself the slightest pleased professional's grin. "250." She finishes what she's writing and snaps the pen in place to the clipboard. "Okay. Now let's get a look-see at those bedrooms."

I haven't indicated where either bedroom is located, but Laura nevertheless leads the way and I follow. Although what was once pert and striking is now merely fit and pretty, the change is for the better, time has done Laura a favour. The streak of premature grey in her hair and the slight sag in her backside are honest at least. Laura's halcyon high-school beauty always seemed slightly phony, like a hundred million dollar promotional budget for a second-rate movie. She unfurls the measuring tape a couple of feet for me to take hold of and walks to the end of my parents' bedroom.

"That house on Wyandot I was talking about?" she says. "The one like this one? I'm happy to say that the seller did quite well, just a little bit under what we were asking."

There may be silver in her hair and a little more flesh on her bones, but I can still hear echoes of cheerleader Laura, even the simplest declarative sentence cadenced into a question. I can almost see her in her white headband and leg warmers while secretly playing with her Rubik's Cube at the back of Mr. Janacek's geography class. "And how much was that?" I say.

"Two-twenty."

Which would certainly be enough to keep Dad nursing-home affluent and then some for the rest of his days. "Let's do it," I say.

"A motivated seller. I like it."

In less than an hour Laura has measured and noted every room and feature in the house and I've given her the okay to list it on her company's website and plant a sign in the front yard. Slowly wrapping what has to be a six-foot-long red scarf around her neck, "And don't worry," she says, "I'm not going to ask you to bake cookies every time a potential buyer shows up."

"I appreciate that."

"But I do think we need to talk about a couple of things that might keep us from getting a deal done as quickly as we both would like and for the price I believe we can get."

"Okay."

"You have to get the furnace turned back on. I can't be expected to sell a house that feels like a meat locker."

I allow myself a moment's silent rebellion. "All right."

"All right. Good."

"What else?" I say.

Laura tucks the end of her scarf into the top of her overcoat and pushes it down, down, until she'll probably need a pair of pliers to get it out. "Understand, I'm not here to judge you, Sam. I'm only here to try and help you sell your house."

"Okay." I cross my arms. And here I thought that the days of Laura Mackenzie looking down her nose at me were over twenty-five years ago. What's next? Coach Duzeria castigating me after football practice for not giving a 110% during tip drills?

"It'll mainly be families I'll be sending your way, and families aren't going to understand empty wine bottles and a bag of weed on the kitchen counter."

"No problem," I say.

"Really?"

"Consider them gone."

"Thanks, Sam. I think we're going to make a good team. I'm really glad Rachel told me you were back in town."

"Rachel Turnbal?"

"The one and the same. We're on the Save CCI Committee together. After she mentioned the other night that she'd run into you, when I saw your name come up on the client list at work I knew it had to be you, so I made sure to snatch you up before someone else did. Us Cougars have got to stick together, right?"

"Right."

Laura kisses the air over both of my cheeks and I let her out. I do what my parents would have done—wait in the doorway and watch her walk to her car—and she turns around on the sidewalk and I open the front door so I can better hear her. "And you should come out to our next meeting. I know you must feel the same way as we all do about saving CCI. And besides, it'd be good for you to see some old familiar faces. You can't spend all of your time cooped up in this house all by yourself."

* * *

BEREAVEMENT PROFESSIONALS TELL YOU that being alone during the holidays is the hardest. Birthdays and anniversaries, too—which, in my case, was especially true, were the only special days of the year Sara and I celebrated, another year still alive and healthy and happy along with another year still together and in love and loving and therefore genuinely worth a special trip to the liquor store for a moderately-priced bottle of chilled Freixenet and a set-aside evening of Sara and Barney and I squeezed onto the couch with me playing vinyl and us being commemoratively giddy-glad we were still here, singularly and plural. I tried to keep up the tradition; I thought it was what Sara would have wanted. But for the record, getting drunk with your dozing dog while deejaying a party of one isn't a particularly effective way of honouring the departed. When Barney was gone less than a year after Sara—such a good dog even to the end, dying just as easy as he lived, a lump on his neck one day and a final visit to the vet three days later—I decided to stop saluting the calendar.

The official days of celebration we rarely bothered with, Christmas included. Christmas particularly. Not being Christians and not wanting to be worse consumers than we already were, we trained both sides of our family to hold the Starbucks gift certificates and the fruit baskets full of Cracker Barrel cheese and bottles of sparkling apple cider and to donate whatever money they'd normally spend on us to the OSPCA, which—along with cheques cut to the United Way and PETA and the World Wildlife Fund—was also our once-yearly way of practising goodwill among men, women, and all the other animals. People would ask us, "Don't you get lonely during the holidays?" but that was actually one of the auxiliary benefits of not preaching what we didn't practice and not pretending that the most logical way of non-religiously celebrating Jesus Christ's birthday was buying all kinds of crap. The neighbourhood sidewalks would thin out, High Park would be wintry empty, the phone would never ring, there was nothing urgent in your inbox that needed replying to. We'd go to Chinatown and eat vegetable chow mein and hot and sour soup and sit with the Jews and all of Toronto's other Christmas delinquents at one of the big movie theatres.

Dining alone at our favourite Chinese restaurant and realizing that bad movies are only fun to watch when there's somebody else with you to laugh at them quickly put an end to those Yuletide rituals as well. This most recent Christmas I was home visiting Dad at Thames View during the holidays, which put me in my parents' house for Christmas Eve, a different, potentially distracting sort of depressing. Apparently Uncle Donny was still paying the house bills back then because the furnace was working and the hot water running. I still don't understand what happened.

I called a taxi and made it to No Frills just before they closed for the night. I bought eggnog and a box of Mandarin oranges and several scented red candles. Then I rushed next door to Blockbuster Video and rented *A Christmas Story*, my mother's and my favourite holiday

TV movie, from way back in those pre-TiVo days when my mum and I would scout the *TV Guide* for its yearly appearance.

I turned off the lights and lit the candles and watched the DVD and drank the entire carton of eggnog and ate so many Mandarin oranges I had a stomach ache that night and the runs all the next day. Even after calling Thames View to check in on Dad, it was only twenty-past-eleven when I decided to go to bed. There was a whole other DVD of *Christmas Story* special features, but I never even took the extra disc out of the case.

* * *

WITH WHAT LITTLE SAVINGS WE'D accumulated in addition to the insurance settlement, I'd done what Sara and I dreamed about but thought would take another fifteen years—paid off our mortgage. We'd always talked about how if we owned our own place we'd have the security that comes from knowing that, no matter how many dogs we might eventually decide to keep as half-crazed childless seniors or how little our combined old-age income might be, no one could tell us what to do, we'd always have a roof over our heads. Except that now that it's ours, it's not ours, it's only mine. I've got a house, but no home.

And after managing to shovel Dad out of the Uncle Donny-dug hole he was in, I've now got my own pecuniary pit to crawl out of. After first arranging it so that all of Dad's pension cheques were diverted back to where they were supposed to be flowing, and then putting his outstanding bill on my credit card, my father is now officially debt-free and back in Thames View's good books. And every month that my parents' house isn't sold I owe the beneficent folks at Visa fifteen-something thousand dollars plus interest that I definitely don't have.

Which is why the first prospective buyer is coming by to look at the house in less than seventy-two hours. Which is why I'm on my knees in the bathroom. With every cleaning-up and clearing-out, however, my parents' house disappears a little bit more. I'm doing what I'm supposed to do, but it feels as if I'm doing something wrong. Each carefully packed cardboard box and rapidly stuffed green garbage bag erases my mother and father just a little bit more. I'm scouring and sorting underneath the bathroom sink when I find the mirror my mother kept for plucking her eyebrows and making sure her hair was okay at the back. When I was a kid, if it was too cold or too hot outside for road hockey or there wasn't anybody at home to ride bicycles around the subdivision with or to stomp through the nearby corn fields with—our GI Joes and Johnny Wests dangling from our hands and ready for action—you had to try and make your own fun. I'd get the mirror from under the bathroom sink and hold it underneath my chin and walk around the house, eyes never leaving the mirror, everywhere I went the opposite of everything the way it usually was. The ceiling was now the floor, and I walked across the ceiling. The light fixtures became obstacles to be avoided, and I either stepped over or around them. Going in and out of doorways was about the same, only now you knew where they were by the doors hanging from the ceiling. When I'd get tired of defeating gravity I'd go find Pepelou, our cat, who would usually be sleeping on the living-room carpet. I'd get down on the floor beside her and nudge her awake, place the mirror in front of her face. The idea was to get her to recognize herself. I'd push the mirror closer, I'd pull it back to give her some perspective, I'd lie down on my stomach and hold the mirror flat on the floor in front of me and get my face in the frame beside hers, but none of it mattered, she just wasn't interested, her eyes would be open but she just couldn't—or wouldn't—see herself.

Too much of this sort of packing will give you a sore back and a sorer heart, so I go to the fridge for a Mountain Dew and pop its top standing at the front window. Surprise, surprise, there are no surprises, 2:16 PM today the same as 2:16 PM yesterday and no doubt tomorrow afternoon at 2:16 PM as well. An empty street and frozen front yards and parked cars *ad infinitum*, notwithstanding the occasional house that hasn't had its Christmas lights taken down yet. I'm almost ready to get back to my garbage bags and boxes when I spot Samantha's father step out of their house and wobble down the sidewalk for his thrice-weekly afternoon liquor store run. I've noticed that he usually gets picked up by a minivan cab earlier in the day—likely DUI-licenceless and wanting to avoid any overlap with either Samantha or her brother returning home from school—but time sure does fly when the glass of straight vodka in your hand makes it difficult to read the watch on your wrist.

He from the end of his sidewalk and I from my living room both see the same thing—a white minivan turning the corner onto Dahlia Avenue. But what I know is just the man next door returning home from his shift at Biddel Tires, Samantha's dad is sure it's his taxi come to take him to the liquor store at the Thames Lee Mall, his tottering steps into the street when he sees my next-door neighbour stopping and backing into his driveway testament to his frustration with this obviously confused cabbie. When he teeters into the middle of the road he stops and wearily waves the reversing minivan his way. When my oblivious neighbor finishes backing all the way in, Samantha's father has had enough, has indulged this fool for as long as he can, puts his hands on his hips and shouts what I can hear through the window, "No, no, no, you're here for me. Do you hear me? Hello? I'm the one who called the cab. Hello? Hello?"

Retreating to the bathroom before this scene plays itself out is a crime against literature, I know, my naturally voyeuristic nose for such an incipient disaster nosed out, however, by the realization that this isn't just some drunk I might be able to utilize for comedic purposes in one of my novels, this is Samantha's father, this is the shit she daily has to live with.

I get back down on my knees and take my mother's hand mirror out of the box intended for Goodwill. Who knows? Maybe I'll end up needing it someday.

*   *   *

"AND HERE'S ONE MORE, JUST ONE MORE. This one is of Francine and Constance, who you've both already seen, but in this one they're with their cousin Priscilla, my brother's daughter. You remember my little brother Tyler, don't you?"

Not really, no, I barely remember you, in fact. "Tyler, right, of course. Your little brother. What was he—one, two years behind us?"

"Hold on a second." Barry Hamilton pleads for my continued patience with a raised forefinger while playing with his phone until he locates the shot he's looking for. Finding it, he pushes the phone six inches from my face. "Not so little now, is he?"

No, he certainly is not. Even if I could recall what Tyler Hamilton looked like twenty-five years ago, I likely wouldn't be able to make the connection between him and the short, rotund, balding, bearded man in the digital photograph that Barry is sticking up my nose.

"The little SOB is down in Toledo in the front office of the biggest safety consulting firm in all of Ohio. They're the number one single supplier of qualified personnel to the Department of Homeland Security in the entire Ohio-Michigan area. The little SOB has got a half-a-million dollar house and a Porsche Carrera GT. Can you believe that?"

Rachel spots me halfway across the gymnasium and manages to say hello without speaking or using her hands, and I tell Barry I'll be right back while giving him a duplicate of the forefinger he'd used to invoke my patience instead of the one I'd much prefer to supply him with, and meet her by the refreshment table.

"You and Barry all caught up now?" she says.

"The only thing more boring than other people's photographs are other people's dreams."

"Oh, I don't know. I've had some dreams recently you might not find so boring."

Common courtesy almost compels me to ask what they are until Rachel's dirty smirk informs me that they're not the sort of dreams one discusses at an information dispensing session in a well-lit high-school gym. I repeatedly dip a tea bag in my Styrofoam cup, but even this seems too forward, as if, in lieu of suggestive hand puppets, I'm doing my best to flirt right back with the limited foodstuffs available. I drop the tea bag in the garbage pail.

"So your community spirit got the best of you after all," Rachel says, swishing a wooden stir stick in her own Styrofoam cup.

"That, and I got tired of cleaning up my parents' house."

"Laura Mackenzie's your real estate agent, I hear."

"I guess I have you to thank for that."

"Or blame."

"She seems okay. Better than when we were all here, anyway."

"A bitch yesterday is a bitch today."

"She wasn't *that* bad." I look over my shoulder to make sure she's not standing behind us.

"Maybe not to you."

A hum of a microphone followed by, "Can we please have everyone take their seats now please?" and everyone does just that, fills the ten or so rows of nicked and dented grey metal folding chairs that we used for school assemblies two decades ago. Instead of *déjà vu*, however, I feel the same thing I felt twenty-five years in reverse, like sneaking out before the boredom begins and there's no chance to get away unnoticed. The woman at the podium thanks us all for coming and someone else for supplying the cookies and someone else for the muffins and by the time she's going over some of the questions that were raised at the last meeting, I'm knee-over-knee, chin-in-hand pretending to pay attention to what she's saying while really studying my fellow Cougar alumni, who are interspersed in the audience with the concerned parents of present CCI students.

It's not who's here that's so absorbing—all of my old teachers are either retired or dead, and most of the people I was closest to back then didn't stick around town too long after graduation—but what happened to the ones that are here: somehow they got old. The men who were boys when I knew them have nearly all capitulated to the twin taunts of thinning hair and receding hairlines and have shaved their heads to varying degrees of bristly clean, so much the better to view their fleshy faces and bushy eyebrows. The girls turned women look like nothing so much as their mothers: short hair, flat shoes, flabby arms. All of which means that I must be old now, too. Forty-four *is* old, I know, but knowing isn't feeling, and feeling, as everyone knows, is how we really come to know something. Seeing silver in all-star point guard and *Reach for the Top* team captain Tommy Anderson's hair—barrister Tommy Anderson, LLB—makes me *feel* old. Discovering that several of my former classmates have children of their own at the very same high school that we attended makes me *feel* old. Learning that Richard Stokowski died of leukemia three years ago makes me *feel* old.

Rachel doesn't make me feel old. Sitting beside me in her Jimmy Choo heels and sleek black skirt and dangling Prada handbag, Rachel makes me—me, in my Levis and Blundstones and short-sleeve western shirt—feel like a lucky lumberjack who's stumbled into the wrong seat but who has yet to be ushered out. But that's in my head—in my nostrils, it's 1980-something and eleven o'clock on Saturday night at someone's house party way out in the country, and it's spring, finally spring, spilt beer and wood smoke and a warm breeze carrying the faintest, surprisingly not unpleasant stink of skunk spray. I uncross then recross my legs, forcing Rachel to do the same.

"Try to stay awake and I'll buy you a Budweiser after this is over," Rachel whispers in my ear. I can't identify her perfume—it's different from Sara's, the only perfume I've nosed first-hand for a long, long time—but it's nice, floral fresh, but not too sweetly chemically strong.

"Make it a Heineken and I'll even sign the petition," I whisper back.

"I thought you were a Bud man."

"Maybe when I used to shoot hoops in here during second period," I say, pointing to the basketball net suspended above us like a low brow mistletoe. Budweiser was just another irresistible US import that, like McDonalds and Hershey chocolate bars, was never as good as it seemed like it would be on the American TV commercials you'd seen for years, even though you couldn't get it in Canada.

"C'mon, where's the fun in having good taste when you're back in your hometown?"

"Fair enough. Tonight, I'm a Bud man."

Rachel pats me on the knee. "Good boy. And not only are you going to sign the petition, you're going to give me a donation by the end of the night too."

In that case, I want to say, it's a good thing you're buying the beer, because at the moment I'm the biggest charity case in this gym. I wonder if Uncle Donny bet on basketball games? Somehow it would be easier to take knowing he lost his brother's shirt betting on a sport he at least knew something about. But that doesn't make any sense. Uncle Donny has been a Maple Leafs fan for fifty-plus years—obviously he doesn't know anything about hockey either.

I listen to the speaker still talking at the podium, and what I hear—annually decreasing enrollment, board of education cost-efficiency, general public apathy—isn't encouraging, although not surprising. The world needs door-to-door canvassers to raise money for the needy and community newspapers to expose scheming local politicians and internet shut-ins to blather honestly about big business shenanigans, and I thank you—the world thanks you—for busying yourself so busily. But my parents never went to church and I never belonged to Boy Scouts and no one ever taught me that city hall could be beaten. It might have been Epictetus who wrote that "Freedom is secured not by the fulfilling of one's desires, but by the removal of desire," but it was my mother who always said, "Oh well, what are you going to do?" Greek stoicism and Chatham working-class indifference aren't all that different, the disparity in the number of undergraduate philosophy courses dedicated to each notwithstanding. I hope a way is found to keep CCI open—it's a good thing, and good things are as desirable as they are uncommon—but I'm not hopeful.

When the podium is empty and the leftover cookies and muffins are packed away and people are putting on their coats and pulling on their gloves and scarves, I stand and slip on my jacket and am aware that I'm waiting for Rachel, who's talking to the presenter and a couple of other people. Am I on a date? No, of course I'm not on a date. I'm just going to the Montreal House with Rachel Turnbal for a beer.

*   *   *

THE NEXT MORNING, AFTER RACHEL dropped me off at home, I get the bucket and rag and Pine-Sol back out and returned to the bathroom to finish what I'd started. I sniffed last night's stale souvenirs of sweat and latex and women's perfume and decided I'd better clean myself before I finished the bathroom.

I knew I hadn't done anything wrong—Sara wouldn't have expected me to take a vow of celibacy—but after I showered and changed and got back down on my knees on the bathroom floor I tugged off my wedding ring and slipped it into my pocket. It wasn't symbolic, I wasn't trying to tell myself something, I didn't feel a sudden release, a dizzying freedom, the bitter sweet beginning of a brand new chapter in my life.

It was time to scour the tub and I was going to use Comet and I didn't want to get my ring dirty or worse. And when I was done and decided to leave it on the table beside the bed—where I'd placed our wedding picture, which I'd transferred from the living room—it was only because I had a lot of cleaning to do before the house was sold and everything I was going to keep was packed away and it made sense to wait until there was nothing left to do before I put it back on.

Chapter Eight

NOW THAT SOMEONE MIGHT SEE me in them, I realize I need new underwear. Underwear and socks. Sometimes life is just that simple.

There are places other than the downtown mall to get what I need, but I knew I'd end up here. It's the same reason I don't choose to buy Heinz Ketchup or Kraft Peanut Butter or Sunlight Dish Soap but always come home with them from the grocery store anyway. My mother bought all of my back-to-school clothes from Sears—first from the catalogue, then in person when the mall opened up around the time I started high school—so that's where I shop, even in Toronto, for all of existence's most essential items. When it was time to replace our fridge or a piece of furniture, Sara would attempt to convince me to at least have a look around the sort of glassy and gleamy Toronto shops that always have a complimentary cappuccino bar and several model-worthy salespersons, but I remained adamant about Sears' sound return policy and reasonable prices. Plus, Sears is where I had my first part-time job, made the money I spent on records and junk food and gas money, my earliest adult purchases. We're loyal to what made us, whether we take an oath or not.

"Sam."

I'm out of the cold and inside the mall and on my way to Sears—near the lottery booth, just past Bed, Bath, and Beyond—when I'm actually relieved that I'm hearing voices. Because I guess I'm just one of those people who isn't made to be mellow, it's time to admit that my attempt to brain-tame myself with weed has been a failure, and who likes to fail at anything? All other arguments against it aside, even if marijuana does seem to encourage metaphysical mellowness and cosmic contemplativeness and the not-unpleasant sensation of not really giving a damn, imagining someone calling out your name in the middle of the afternoon does seem a rather high price to pay in return.

"Sam. Over here."

Except that now it appears as if I'm *not* hearing things—a not-so-young, not-so-old (my age, if I think about it) couple loaded down with assorted shopping bags like two overworked mules hear what I hear too, look where I'm looking also. Except that the voice calling out my name is emanating from a very large, very furry squirrel handing out leaflets in front of the Bank of Montreal. Either the couple has been smoking the same weed as I have or that's a squirrel costume with someone inside it who knows my name. I don't have time to consider which proposition is the more frightening.

"Sam, it's me, Scott." The squirrel points a paw at himself. I come closer, but without managing to crack the rodent code. With both paws gesturing toward himself now, including the one holding the leaflets, "Me, Scott Frampton."

Scott "Frampton Comes Alive" Frampton.

There's always the slightly older guy who isn't good at sports and isn't good at school and isn't, truth be told, the sharpest knife in the drawer, but who makes up for it all by possessing that most coveted of items—a car—and Scott was him when I was at CCI. It was his mother's car, actually—a blue 1977 Monte Carlo—and being friends with Scott meant that on Friday or Saturday night you'd look for his headlights flashing through the sheer curtains in the living room or listen for the crunch of stone underneath his tires in the driveway. Your coat would be on and your wallet was in your back pocket and you'd already promised your parents you'd be home by one o'clock, and when Scott pulled into the driveway you could breathe normally again and hurry to the door and then coolly walk to the Monte Carlo, hoping to ride shotgun but happy to just have a seat. Just because he said he'd pick you up didn't mean he was going to actually show, the agony of watching eight PM become 8:15 (he's just late), then 8:30 (call his house but he's already left), then 8:45 (coat off, but not put away in the closet yet), then 9:10 and moping in front of the TV and your dad asking if you wanted a ride and you answering no, because it wasn't about anywhere in particular you were supposed to be, it was all about going.

"Hey, Scott," I say, instinctively offering him five fingers before realizing that squirrels don't shake hands. Scott bumps his paw against my fist.

"What the fuck are you doing back here in Chatham, you fucker?" he says without pausing from his labours, which seem to consist in handing out flyers detailing the bank's assorted saving accounts, all of which guarantee interest rates so attractively high, you'll be able to save your hard-earned money like the world's most frugal—and largest—squirrel.

"Just visiting. You know."

"Hey, I heard you're a writer or something. Mum says she sees you in the *Globe and Mail* sometimes."

"Sometimes, yeah. Sometimes when I write something for them." Which is so tautologically obvious it makes very little sense, although it suffices for Scott, who nods his massive squirrel head several times in understanding. Out of respect for the many times he did show up as promised in the Monte Carlo and saved me from a Friday night watching *Fantasy Island* followed by an episode of *Hart to Hart* with my mum, I don't ask Scott what he's been up to for the last couple of decades.

"Well, I better get going, but it's good to see you again, Scott."

"Fuck, yes, Sam. We should get a fucking brew sometime. Get caught up."

"Absolutely."

"I'm in the book."

"Right."

"The phone book."

"Right."

"So don't be a fucking stranger and call me."

"Okay. I will."

"And don't work too hard. You fucker, you."

"Right. You too."

While getting what I need from the menswear section at Sears I remember why Scott dropped out of CCI and why we lost touch. Airplane glue *is* substantially cheaper and easier to acquire on a Saturday night at eleven than a twelve pack of Canadian, but it does come with side-effects slightly more debilitating than the premature development of a belt-high Molson muscle. After I get my underwear and socks I give in to the mall's somnolent flow, eventually find myself at Coles, where I learn that Chatham's only bookstore doesn't carry any of my books, but does have an ample supply of Nora Roberts and Tom Robbins novels.

I'm on my way out of the store when I almost don't recognize Samantha, so used to always seeing her packed into her winter jacket. She's sitting by herself at a table for two in the food court eating a piled-high plate of poutine while listening to her iPod and reading what looks like a fat textbook. I stay where I am, just inside the entrance to the bookstore, until I realize that someone could easily misconstrue what I'm doing as watching her. When she looks up from her book to brush a long strand of hair out of her face and behind her right ear, she recognizes me, seems as surprised to see me here as I am her. I return *The History of the Electric Guitar* back to the shelf and walk over. She thumbs something on her iPod but doesn't remove her ear buds. I motion with my chin toward the book.

"How can you concentrate in here?"

She shrugs. "I'm usually listening to music."

"How can you concentrate with music on?"

She shrugs again. They should call her generation *Generation Shrug*. "It's just physics."

"And what kind of music goes best with physics?"

"At the moment, Jim Bryson." She can tell I have no idea who that is. "He's sort of neo-folk. Sort of a post modern singer-songwriter. Don't feel bad—even if you did occasionally listen to people who were actually still alive, you probably wouldn't know his stuff. He's pretty underground."

"Do you know who Jim Osterberg is?"

"No."

"As it is written, a Jim for Jim. I guess we're even then."

She pulls out her right ear bud and offers it to me. "Do you want to check out what my Jim sounds like?"

"Pass," I say, picking up her textbook instead. The cover is different from the copy I had in high school, but inside is familiarly incomprehensible. "I dropped physics," I say, thumb-flipping through to the end. You forget sometimes—there *are* compensations for growing old. Like not having to understand how the universe works.

"Why did you drop it?"

Closing the book and putting it back on the table, "I was failing."

"Really." She seems genuinely surprised that anyone could be so dim; curious even, like a psychologist might wonder at a child who has difficulty fitting round blocks into round holes.

"Let's just say my strengths were elsewhere," I say.

"What, like phys-ed?"

"No, like … " I stop before I threaten to march home and get my grade thirteen report card.

Samantha drinks from her can of Diet Coke through a straw. "What's in the bag?"

"Just towels," I say, swinging the Sears bag behind my back. Not that shopping for underwear and socks is anything to be embarrassed about. "I ran out of towels."

"I meant to ask you. If your hot water heater isn't hooked up, how do you get water to take a shower?"

"Actually, I just got it turned back on. Before that, I took baths. I just dumped a few kettles worth of boiling water in with the cold water."

"It might have been easier to have just gotten the gas turned on when you got here."

"I didn't think I was going to be here long enough for it to be worth it."

"And you do now?"

"I guess. Maybe not. I don't know." Wanting to both change the subject and have someone listen to me gripe, "I asked the kid working in menswear if they had any blue jeans that didn't fall apart like these"—I point to three separate dime-sized holes that have sprouted in the expensive pair of jeans I bought in Toronto less than six months ago—"and he asked me how often I washed them. 'Whenever they're dirty,' I said, and he said, 'Oh, you can't do that with good blue jeans. Only wash them, like, every two months, max.'" When I don't see the head-shaking confirmation of the absurdity of teenage sales staffers/ modern manufacturing values I was looking for, I deliver the cuckoo *coup de grace*: "So I asked him, 'If I don't wash them, what do I do when they start to smell?' You know what he said to me?"

"Put them in the freezer?" Samantha says.

I give up, shake my own head. This is why we have friends our own age. So we can complain and commiserate about people younger than us.

Samantha pokes her white plastic fork into the swamp of brown crud covering her Styrofoam plate. Before I can get too Thou Shalt Not, though, I remember that I used to sit where she's sitting now, used to take my lunch break at this very food court when I worked at Sears. Mr. Pong's was my preferred half-hour destination, what the three chicken balls that came with the Number Two Lunch Special lacked in chicken they more than made up for with plenty of deep-fried dough and sweet orange sauce. And compared to kids today, who can't even remember a time before recycling, my teenage carbon footprint is probably deeper than hers and all of her classmates combined.

"This is lunch," she says. "I've got class in twenty minutes."

"Go ahead."

Lifting her fork, "You said you don't eat meat anyway, right?"

"Even if I still did, I wouldn't be eating that." Yes I would. Christ, since when did I start sounding like my mother?

On the way to her mouth an overloaded forkful of poutine plops onto her left forearm; in the process of grabbing for her napkin, she knocks over the can of Diet Coke which soaks the same shirt sleeve.

"See?" I say. "Karma."

"Do you believe in karma?"

"No. But I do believe you're going to need some more napkins."

When I return from the A&W counter Samantha has pulled up her shirt sleeve and is doing her best to wring it dry. There are sharp red welts travelling all the way down from her elbow to just above her wrist.

"You didn't get those from spilling poutine," I say, offering her the napkins but still staring at the scars on her forearm.

"Asshole," she says, yanking down her shirt sleeve. "Asshole stalker spy."

"Hey, c'mon," I say, looking around to see if anyone heard her. I'm still holding out the napkins, although she's busy yanking on her coat and grabbing her books. "Sorry," I say, although for what, I'm not sure.

I follow her through the food court and down the escalator and onto King Street, but without calling out her name or imitating her half-jog. Even asshole stalker spies have their dignity. I decide not to trail her all the way to CCI, as forty-four year-old pursuant men on high-school property are never a good combination, regardless

of their appeasing intentions. She crosses against traffic—
narrowly avoiding a honking pick-up truck—and I watch
her go.

* * *

DING DONG AND HELLO HELLO, and is this the original roof
and are the fridge and stove included and what are your
hydro and gas bills like in the wintertime and how old is
the roof and what type of foundation is it and does the
house have insulation in the walls and attic and what are
the schools around here like and how much are the property taxes and how long has the house been on the market
and how do you find your neighbours?

By walking out the front door, I want to say. Real estate
etiquette dictates that ordinarily I wouldn't even be here
while Laura was showing the house, but apparently the
prospective owners requested that I be present so that they
could get a horse's mouth yea or neigh regarding the child-
friendly nature of the neighbourhood.

"Like I said, it's my parents' house and I didn't grow
up here, but from what I can tell, the neighbours are very
quiet, I haven't heard a peep from anyone since I've been
around. And there's the park next door which would be
great for kids." When no one's using it to guzzle wine or
smoke pot, anyway.

"Uh huh, uh huh, right, right." The woman, the one
asking all the questions, marches off with Laura, clipboard
in hand, to have another look at something in one of the
bedrooms, the man staying behind with me in the living
room. Laura made coffee and brought donuts and the husband and I sit on either end of the sofa while the adults
go about their mysterious adult business. If only the man

would ask me about the house, we'd have something to talk about, even if I really don't have any answers.

Instead, grinning, "Records, eh?" he says, gesturing with his coffee cup at my eBay purchase, five records received in the morning mail, leaning against the living room wall. "Haven't seen any of those in a while."

He's younger than me, but not by much, likely first-time house-hunting, the calloused, scaly hand I'd shaken half an hour earlier testament to a good-paying factory job. For now, at least.

"I can't really afford it, but there were a couple of things I couldn't pass up. And once you get your credit card out..." And once you already owe the credit card company fifteen thousand dollars plus interest, what's $150 more?

"Where's your record player? Didn't know they still made 'em."

"I don't have one." The man looks confused. "Not here, I mean. I have one at home. Two, actually." The man looks alarmed. "Home in Toronto, I mean."

"Oh, right." The man looks relieved, then embarrassed. "You're here because of your...your family business."

Laura must have filled them in, probably didn't spare them a single familial tragedy, hoping, no doubt, that their heartstrings will get tangled up with their purse strings. I just nod into my empty coffee cup a couple of times. The man does the same.

Looking up, "But now you've got to take your albums all the way home with you," he says. "Too bad you couldn't have bought them when you were there."

"I couldn't take the risk of someone else getting them."

The man grins. "Good ones?"

"Real good ones."

Which they are; but, except for Willie P. Bennett's *Tryin' to Start Out Clean*, a copy of which I already own, nothing so special I couldn't have waited to buy once I'm back in Toronto. Buying records, particularly rare, expensive records on eBay, is something I haven't done since Sara died. I bought these five last week after talking with Samantha in the park. Drinking wine and talking with Samantha in the park. The internet equivalent of drunk dialing, I suppose.

I hear "perfect for a nursery" and "but the sun in the morning" and Laura and the woman are back. The man sets his cup on the coffee table and stands up. I follow suit, stretch, and manage to spot Samantha's dad wobbling down the middle of the street at 10:30 in the morning, a red-nosed, gargantuan baby in a flapping-open grey overcoat just learning to get from here to there without tipping. From what I've observed over the last few weeks from the snooping perch of my parents' front window, he's either up-and-out-of-the-house-at-seven-AM sober or scarcely-vertical plastered, his obviously senior position at his law firm meaning that the underlings who occasionally come by with papers for him to sign when he's too tanked to make it into the office are occupationally compelled to ignore the stumbling elephant in the room. Laura's the certified real estate agent, but I know a deal-breaker when I see one, so announce a little too enthusiastically, "You haven't seen the shed yet."

Which does cause everyone to turn and look at me, but which also keeps everyone from looking out the front window. I'm talking ("There's room enough for a lawnmower *and* a snow blower if you didn't want to keep them in the garage, which you could also do") while simultaneously watching Samantha's dad almost make it inside his house before stopping short and swaying in place, as if teetering

131

in the bitter breeze. C'mon, just a little further, keep moving, keep moving…

"Well, great, that's good to know, Sam, thanks," Laura says, clapping and clasping her hands and pulling the attention back to her. "And do you two have any other questions?" The man and the woman look at each other, Laura looks at me like she hopes whatever's suddenly taken possession of me can somehow be suppressed for at least a few more minutes, I look out the window trying not to seem like I'm looking out the window, Samantha's dad now stationary, but with his nose in the air like a scent-smitten hound. Until Samantha's brother bursts through the door and nearly bumps him off the step, eyes down and knapsack slung over his shoulder and both thumbs busy texting. Samantha's dad looks more bewildered than upset, like he can't quite believe his son didn't see him when passing less than a foot from his face.

"No, I think we're good," the woman says, smiling and nodding at the man who takes his cue and does the same.

"Well, okay, then," Laura says, sticking out her hand. "It's been great meeting you both, and you've got my card and number if there's anything else you need from our end." Handshakes, smiles, and thank yous, and we just make it, Samantha's father closes his door behind him and we're all a happy neighbourhood again.

Laura and I walk the man and the woman to their car and wave them off, and if they do notice Samantha's father looking out of his front window at Samantha's brother, all they would see is a father watching his son walk to school, the latter perhaps paying a little too much attention to the text he's reading and not enough to where he's going.

* * *

YOU DON'T NEED DARWIN TO KNOW that human beings are foremost fornicators. Just observe a married man suffer a room full of attractive women, his wedding ring suddenly a cramping, unnatural appendage. And fucking really *is* like riding a bicycle, all you need to do is climb right back on and pump away and enjoy the ride. As odd as it is being with a woman again, it's odder still being with a woman who isn't yours. Your woman with her singular smells and preferred positions and inimitable loving ways.

"Making yourself at home, I see," Rachel says, padding into her apartment's small kitchen, back in her jeans and sweater, a white towel wrapped around her head, barefoot and shower-fresh. I stay where I am, kneeling in the adjacent living room in front of the black plastic CD tree next to the small bookshelf that, though white and made of thin plywood, looks as if it was purchased from the same store, the kind of place that sells not only cheap furniture for lonely single professionals, but scented candles and pot-pourri bowls and just about everything else no one really needs. Instead of books, one of the shelves is covered with neat piles of Keep-CCI-Open petitions, safe-copy Xeroxes of the real thing.

"Just checking to see if your musical taste has evolved over the last twenty-five years."

"I'm pretty sure I hid all of the Duran Duran CDs when I knew you were coming over. Find something you like and put it on, okay? I'm going to start dinner."

Sara cooked and I did the dishes, but Sundays I was mostly on my own, Sara lengthwise on the couch with a paperback novel and dinner not even a consideration until the last page was turned, usually no earlier than seven or eight PM. We didn't go to church and there were no big family dinners to attend and we weren't the sort of couple to meet friends for brunch, but Sundays were Sundays because Sara was not to be bothered until she was finished reading her Sabbath day paperback.

"How does a pork chop and a salad sound?" Rachel says.

"Actually, I don't eat pork."

"Okay." Rachel opens up the refrigerator, looks inside. "How about if I throw together a chicken stir fry?"

"I don't actually eat chicken, either."

Rachel lets the fridge door close on its own. "What do you eat then? Actually."

I stand up from my snooping stoop. "Look, don't worry about it, okay? I didn't expect dinner to be a part of the deal anyway."

"And what deal is that specifically?"

What deal indeed. "I just meant that we're just—"

"Just what? Just fuck buddies?"

"No. That's not what I said."

"It's not what you said, but it's obviously what you meant. Which is fine. It's completely fine. I'd just like it if we were both on the same page, is all."

"Look, I ... I just don't eat meat, okay?"

Rachel lets her eyes linger on me for a long moment before re-opening the fridge door. "What about vegetables? Do you actually eat vegetables?"

"I have been known to eat some of those occasionally."

She starts pulling carrots and celery and red and green peppers out of the fridge. "One chicken stir-fry minus the chicken coming up."

"That sounds great. Can I do anything to help?"

"Why don't you carry on with what you were doing?"

"You got it."

I kneel back down and study every CD spine from top to bottom, then start all over again; if only there *were* some Duran Duran. What's musically worthless might at least be good for some nostalgic groans, a little Auld Lang Syne self-aimed laughter. What we have instead is plenty of Blue Rodeo and Tragically Hip and Dave Matthews and, for those more introspective moments, Sarah McLachlan and Tori Amos and Alanis Morissette. If you can't love, you should at least be able to hate, but all I feel is boredom. I'm almost ready to suggest we turn on the dishwasher and listen to that instead when I spot Tom Waits' *Rain Dogs*. I slip it into the CD player and head to the kitchen.

"Can I at least set the table?" I say.

"Sure. The plates are right to your left, second cupboard."

"Got it."

"Before you do that, though, would you do me a favour?'

"Shoot."

"Put another CD on, would you? It doesn't matter what, just as long as it's not this. One of the teachers at school made me borrow it from her and I've been avoiding bringing it back for months now because I don't know what to say. I don't want to hurt her feelings, but, I mean, is this guy for real or what? Didn't anyone ever suggest to him that a singing lesson or two might be a good idea if you're going to be a singer? Hello?"

* * *

FIRST I HEAR IT, ALTHOUGH WHAT *it* is isn't clear. I go to the living room window and slap my way through the sheers and see that it's just the fat man from before on his tiny mini-bike chugging around the block, the sound of a tired tug boat panting its way to shore. Except that he doesn't disappear around the corner but turns back at street's end, all the better for his almost identically blue snowsuit-outfitted fat girlfriend or wife to capture on video the heroic putt-putt up and down the street. He waves at her on the way by and she pivots right around so as not to miss an instant of his virtually seat-swallowing ass travelling the other way. I wish there was someone here to witness what I'm seeing, and then there is, there's Samantha standing on her front step, jacket undone and running shoes unlaced. I haven't seen her since she ran away from me at the mall. I step out onto my front step.

"The call of the wild," I shout.

In spite of herself, she smiles—sort of. Doesn't answer, however. I know I've got my work cut out for me.

Seeing that the woman working the digital camera is also listening to an iPod, I feel it's safe to ask, "How long do you think before it shows up on YouTube?"

Samantha folds her arms across her chest, but I don't think it's because she's cold. She's not going anywhere, though. Not yet. I'd better work fast.

"I've got something for you," I say.

"What?"

"I want to give it to you."

"That's kind of usually what happens when you've got something for someone, isn't it?"

"I mean I don't want to ruin the surprise."

"I hate surprises."

"Everyone likes surprises."

"I'm not everyone."

"Just come over. It'll only take a minute."

She looks at her running shoes. I want to tell her to do up her laces or she'll trip, but I don't want to sound like

136

my father. Without looking up, "How do I know you're not going to cut me up into fifty pieces and stick them in your freezer?" she says.

"I'm a vegetarian, remember? Besides, my parents' freezer is full of about two hundred pounds of frozen cow parts. I simply don't have any room for any Homo sapiens at the moment."

This time she does smile, if begrudgingly. "I've got to get something inside. I'll be over in a minute."

While Samantha retrieves the something that I know is her pot, I've got to make good on my promise of a gift. She doesn't have a record player, so nothing in this morning's eBay delivery will suffice. My mother's Swiffer Duster? A sample of her choice from Mum's miniature spoon collection? One of Dad's several screwdriver sets? When she simultaneously knocks and enters, I spot my salvation just in time. "There she is," I say, picking up and holding out to her what every eighteen-year-old girl simply can't get by without.

"Thanks."

"You're welcome."

We both stare at what she's holding.

"Don't think I'm not grateful," she says.

"But?"

"But what is it?"

"It's a paper shredder," I say.

"Oh."

"You know. For shredding paper."

"Okay."

We both stare at the paper shredder.

"It's so people don't get a hold of your mail or anything with your personal information on it. Apparently, identity theft is a growing problem among the elderly."

"The elderly."

"Or the young. The young too. It's never too soon to start safe-guarding against identity theft."

"Well, thanks."

"You're welcome."

We both stare at Samantha's new paper shredder.

"I'm going to get high," she says.

"I think that's a very good idea."

While Samantha settles back on the couch and pulls out her weed and rolling papers, I turn up the thermostat. "I think I told you I got the heat turned back on," I say. "You can take your coat off if you want." I know I've said what I shouldn't have said as soon as I say it. The whole point of inviting her over is to subtly coax her into talking about the scars I saw, so appearing as if I'm trying to sweat her out of her coat in order to expose the evidence is the wrong move. I won't be surprised if she flees me again.

Instead, "You told me. But why did you do it? I thought you didn't want to feel too settled."

"The real estate agent said I needed to if she's going to be able to sell the house."

"Was that the blonde in the red minivan?"

"Aren't you ever at school?"

"When I need to be." Samantha slips the readied joint between her lips; makes it crackle alive with the flame from her lighter and a sharp intake of breath that turns the joint's end orange, expert stoner alchemy.

"Speaking of," I say. "What universities did you apply to?" If the front door to the present is presently off limits, maybe I can bluff my way in through the back.

"How do you know I applied to any?"

Because you're eighteen years old and living in Chatham, Ontario, with your drunk of a father and your fourteen-year-old brother. Because when I was your age and living in Chatham, Ontario, I couldn't wait to leave, had literally worn out the guidance office's copy of the University of Toronto calendar, the once-glossy cover thumbed dull and the endlessly turned pages falling out by the time my acceptance letter finally arrived in the mail in the spring.

"Okay," I say. "*Have* you applied to any universities?"

"I've applied to a few."

"You don't sound too excited."

"I never said I was."

"Don't you think you should be?"

"I don't know. Should I?"

Instead of beginning, *When I was your age . . .* , "Is U of T one of them?" I ask.

"One of the ones I applied to?"

"Yeah."

"I don't think so."

"You don't *think* so?"

"I can't remember. It was like three months ago when I filled out the form."

"I know, but . . . " But now I'm starting to understand why your right hand has sprouted an extra appendage in the form of the joint that's perpetually stuck there and why you may very well have self-inflicted cut wounds on your arms. "But you should have applied to U of T as well. For one thing, you'd love Toronto."

"I told you, I'm from Toronto."

"Right, I forgot." Forgot that Oakville still spells Toronto to her, the latter of which she really would love once she got to know it: antiquarian bookstores with signed Virginia Woolfs and Jack Kerouacs and Walt Whitmans you could never afford to buy but it's thrilling all the same just to know that someone in your very own city can and will; Nigerian taxi drivers who listen to the BBC World News in their cabs and who can make sound arguments for Canada's military withdrawal from the world stage; wonderfully crazy street scholars running around town armed with thick black markers correcting the spelling and grammatical mistakes of their fellow graffitists; a city, in short, too expensive, too crowded, too stuck up, and much too much alive for you to risk missing out on being alive there and being a part of it all.

Instead of saying any of this, though, I tell her how big U of T is and how it can offer so many different kinds of programs and courses and how its library is the nation's largest and how much money it has for scholarships and guest speakers and how many well-known writers and thinkers and scientists are part of its alma mater. I also tell her how even my mum was happy I was going away to university, just not so happy that the university turned out to be in Toronto, not after she and my father helped me move into residence, the first time in the big city for any of us. The ego-dwarfing buildings; the undeniable energy in the streets; all of the people who didn't look like her—none of this boded well for her only baby boy. *It smells like curry*, she said once we'd gotten me settled in my room. *What does?* I said. *Everything*, she said.

"Okay, okay," Samantha says. "Enough with the hard sell. You made your point. I'll add it to the stupid list."

"If it's not too late. You need to talk to your guidance counsellor."

"Okay, I will."

"Right away. It might be too late."

"All right, all right." She relights her joint; inhales; exhales. "So," she says. "Who died tonight?"

So why do you have cuts all down your arm? I want to answer. I realize I have no idea what I'm doing, that I'm in way over my head. There were good reasons, after all, besides ecological farsightedness and simple personal selfishness why Sara and I never had children. I'm in the story business, I'll tell her a story, that might make her feel better. Will certainly make me feel better.

"John Hartford died tonight," I say. "But this one has a happy ending, I promise. If John Hartford's music was about anything, it was happiness. Except that's not the right word—happiness isn't a big enough word. *Joy*. John Hartford's music was about joy. *Is* about joy, I mean. Is."

I sit down on the other end of the couch, lean back for the long haul; the living as well as the dead are counting on me this time.

"John Hartford was born in New York in 1937 to a prominent surgeon and his wife, but grew up in St. Louis, Missouri, where he worked on the Mississippi River as a teenager and listened to the Grand Ole Opry on the radio, Earl Scrugg's brand-new three-finger banjo playing technique the road to Damascus sound that got him walking on his life's plucking path. By the age of thirteen he was an accomplished fiddler and banjo player and led his own high-school bluegrass band."

"I bet that got him a lot of action."

My instinct is to dismiss her sass with a choice anecdote about Hartford's late-'60s Hollywood lady's man days, but then I remember that his song "The First Girl I Loved" was written about his cousin. I motion for the joint instead so she'll feel like I'm with her, not against her; puff, pass it back. I'll have to work fast, will have to talk Hartford back to life before the fervour-flattening effect of the pot takes hold.

"He dropped out of university, he worked as a disc jockey, he played in country and western bands for drunks and tips, and he began writing songs that were one part bluegrass, one part Beatles, one part post-beatnik wit and wisdom, and in 1966 he signed with RCA and came up with his first album, *John Hartford Looks at Life*. The six records he made for RCA over the next five years are lovely and funny and never less than inimitably hummy, but can't help being what they are: albums recorded for a major record label in the late 1960s by a very idiosyncratic musician and songwriter who nonetheless was recording for a major record label in the late 1960s." Samantha offers me the joint; I don't want it, but I take it, toke, hand it back. "There's no such thing as revolution from within. If you lie down with dogs, you're going to get fleas."

"There are dogs who would find that offensive, I bet."

"No doubt."

I lean even further back and sink into the couch as deep as I can; here comes the important part, the part Samantha needs to hear. That everyone needs to hear.

"The first song on side two of Hartford's second album is a song called 'Gentle on My Mind,' which Glen Campbell heard and thought was catchier than the flu and could be a hit if sufficiently polished and pimped, and he was right—it won four Grammies and went on to become one of the most widely recorded songs of all time. More important though than helping to serenade elevators and dentists' offices around the world were the royalties it brought in that allowed Hartford to quit his various day jobs and leave L.A. and move to a home in Tennessee on the Cumberland River and make the kind of music he'd begun to hear in his head. He hired the best pickers around—Vassar Clements on fiddle, Tut Taylor on dobro, Norman Blake on guitar—and in 1971 created *Aereo-Plain*, which sounds like smoking hash out of an old corncob pipe, or, if you prefer, Paul McCartney being molested by Flatt and Scruggs."

"I don't. I definitely don't prefer."

"Smoking hash out of an old corncob pipe it is then."

"Translation, please."

"Meaning that the album begins with a faithful version of its only cover tune—'Turn Your Radio On,' an old gospel call-to-angelic-arms song—before sneaking into 'Steamboat Whistle Blues,' another verse-verse-chorus corker delivered pickin' and strummin' style but which, if you stop humming long enough to really listen, isn't just some old-timey sing-a-long but is actually about how the food we eat is processed and the news we're allowed to hear is processed and the buildings we live in all look the same and that the only thing you can trust these days is an antebellum steamboat plodding off down the river. This is post-Manson-murder music—wilted flower-power music—made by a hippie with a head on his shoulders, somebody who knows that to forget the past is just as foolish as being afraid of the future. Hand me that joint, will you?" I'm almost at the finish line; nothing can slow me down now.

"Maybe you should slow down," Samantha says. She's looking at me like Sara used to look at me when the words couldn't come fast enough to say all they had to say.

"I thought you hated mellow," I say.

"In moderation."

Taking the joint from her, "You know what William Blake said about moderation."

"Hold on. Is that this Hartford guy's guitar player?"

"Now that would be a duo that even Lennon and McCartney would have had a hard time competing with." I only take a quick hit before handing it right back.

"And because it didn't matter anymore if *Billboard* magazine liked it or not or whether he ever got invited to perform on *Hee Haw*, *Aereo-Plain* could comfortably be what it wanted to be: full of songs about falling in love with first cousins and being too dope-paranoid to talk on the telephone and the insanity of modern urban planning and the enduring value of friendship and family and wide open spaces and even acapella odes to the wonderful word 'boogie.'"

"You're kidding, right?"

"Why would I kid around about something like that?" Her joint has gone out now, but she makes no move to relight it. She's listening.

"*Morning Bugle* came next and was much the spectacular same, while 1976's *Mark Twang* was just like it sounds, with the added aural oddity of Hartford accompanying himself alone on banjo or fiddle or whatever other instrument the tune at hand required—on one song it's just him and his cheek—plus, for rhythmical accompaniment, periodic clogging."

"Pardon my ignorance, but—"

"But what's clogging?" I'm on my feet and approximating Hartford's stylish stomping before her sentence is finished. Still moving my feet, "Hartford and his wife and a driver who doubled as the sound man would tour all over North America by this time on a bus with just his banjo and fiddle and guitar and a four foot by eight foot piece of A-grade plywood that he'd use for clogging." I stop, but don't sit back down. "And keep this in mind: everyone goes on and on about the Sex Pistols' album being such a punk watershed, about how its aesthetic is so raw and primitive and DIY. But Steve Jones laid down *weeks* of electric guitar overdubs on that thing and its budget came in at well over a hundred grand. Compared to *Mark Twang*, which was released a whole year earlier, *Never Mind the Bollocks* sounds like L.A. session hacks backed up by the London Philharmonic."

I realize I'm standing in the middle of the living room. I'm a little uncomfortable, just like you always are when you tell someone the truth.

"So he was married?"

"Happily. For many, many years."

"And he didn't shoot heroin into his eyeball or anything?"

"Enjoyed a quality puff and the occasional pint of cider, but nothing that didn't make the music sound better and every moment more alive."

"He doesn't sound like he was too concerned with being a neglected genius or whatever."

"Was too busy having a good time to worry too much about it, I guess."

I'm suddenly very tired, like after an hour of good love making or like coming back to your own bed after a pleasant but long trip. In spite of the furnace blowing out warm air, Samantha still has her jacket on, but at some point she's taken off her running shoes and tucked her feet underneath her on the couch. She looks sleepy too. Then she doesn't; looks instead like she's just woken up late for an important exam and there's no way she's going to make it in time.

"What happened to him?" she says.

"You know what happened to him."

She looks at me; I look at the floor.

"Why?" she says.

"Why what?"

"Why does every story have to end this way?"

"I don't know. They just do."

"No they don't."

"Yeah, they do."

Neither of us says anything else or even moves—is ever going to move. They're going to find us here in the spring in these exact same positions. I look up.

"When Hartford's widow gave the mortician the bag containing the suit she wanted him buried in, somehow his prized Batman cape got mixed up in there. The mortician was obviously a little surprised when he opened up the bag at the funeral home, but figured that since the deceased was an artist, it was probably what his widow wanted. People showed up for the viewing the next day and were understandably a little taken aback, but Hartford's widow took one look and laughed. "Leave it," she said. "John would have loved it.""

CHAPTER NINE

THE STAFF AT THAMES VIEW DO everything they can, but they can't do everything. Like trim errant ear hairs, for example. Every resident receives a monthly haircut whether he needs it or not, but unsightly ear hair or over-grown eyebrows are, if anyone's, the family's responsibility. And no matter how dirty his work clothes were at the end of the day or how much grease ended up underneath his fingernails, those same clothes and nails were always work-day-ready clean whenever he left the house, and nose hairs were tweezered and eyebrows trimmed with just as much weekly dutifulness as Friday's banking and Saturday's trip to the beer store. I'd made Uncle Donny promise to pick up the plucking and trimming slack once Dad wasn't capable anymore, and he'd kept his promise. Now that's he's *persona non Donny*, however, it's my turn to take up the tweezers.

The bus takes nearly half an hour to get to Thames View, but at least there's a stop directly across the street. Before I visit Dad I have a word with Mrs. Hampton about how best to go about hiring a part-time nurse to do all of the little things that Uncle Donny used to do and I presently am but one day I won't be able to, except when I come back to visit. As soon as the house is sold and my

Visa debt is paid off, everything that's left over is going into an account to pay for the part-time nurse and the cable bill and anything else Dad needs. I did the math, and Dad will never outlive the money from the house sale.

I'm stomping any remaining slush water from my boots onto the mushy black mat just outside Dad's room when I see the elderly woman with the cane, the one who I'd thought whacked me with it, shuffling down the corridor, cane in one hand, a handful of bright red cards gripped in the other. I'm wondering whether I should ask her if she needs any help, when I'm saved, a young woman wearing a Thames View nametag hurries behind her down the hall.

"Mrs. Evans," she says, "you know all those cards don't belong to you. Now please give them to me."

The old woman stops, looks at the mess of red missives in her hand, says, "I'm sorry. I don't know how that happened."

"That's all right. But those Valentines are for everyone. You need to remember to share."

"I'm sorry."

"That's all right. Now, can you get back to your room all right?"

"Yes."

"All right then, off you go."

I smile at the old woman as I pass—hopefully not *too* sympathetically—wishing that I'd remembered it was Valentine's Day next week and that I was in the habit of carrying a surplus of cards to distribute to the lonely and long-forgotten, when she curls an arthritis-knotted finger my way.

Softly, but perfectly clearly, "My coffin is much nicer than hers," she says.

"Okay."

"That bitch."

"Right."

"That fucking bitch." And then, for emphasis, she cracks me across my shin with her cane.

Rubbing my leg, Look on the bright side, I think. At least now I know I wasn't imagining it the first time.

"Good evening."

It's Jean, one of Thames View's care workers, come to help Dad back to bed and settle him in for the night. Almost every evening after dinner I try to mix things up a bit by having us change places, prop Dad up in his chair for a short vertical vacation while I sit on the bed. Jean greets every resident with the same congenial, yet never syrupy good morning or good afternoon or good evening, but this time I think she's speaking to me.

"Hello." I stand up from the bed, ready to assist in any way I can, although I know I likely won't be needed. Jean is short and squat—almost square—with plump, veiny forearms and powerful, bowed legs.

"And where is Mr. Samson this evening?" I look at my dad, then back at her—math was never my best subject, but I've always been able to count to two with virtually no outside help.

Seeing my confusion, "Mr. Samson's brother," she says. "I'm not used to tucking Mr. Samson in without his brother being here."

Jean's been on vacation for the last few weeks, and this, I know, is where I'm supposed to explain where Uncle Donny is. Instead, I ask, "Do you need a hand with ... ?" With lugging my cement-sack of a father into bed, the same man whose back I once-upon-a-time used to giddily ride on, whose biceps I would delightfully dangle from, whose mat of thick black chest hair seemed as much of what a man could ever hope to be as anything I could possibly imagine?

With one hand stuck firmly underneath his right armpit and the other wrapped tight around the small of his back, Jean addresses my dad, not me, with "Ready, Mr. Samson? Here we go now: one, two, three, four," and dances my puppet father one-step, two-step, all the way to the edge of the bed, where, just like he's supposed to, he sits and stares and waits for his housecoat and slippers to be removed. If melancholic reflections upon the tragic passing of time are what you're after, a writer is the right person for the job; if, however, you want your moribund father to be efficiently and safely moved from Point A to Point B, ask a patient care worker.

First the slippers, left then right, then the housecoat, then carefully but firmly laying him back and tucking him in, then the hard survey to ensure that everything is as it should be. I watch Jean watch my dad, thankful that another day is done, thankful that Jean is watching over him. By the way she remains standing there, though, hands-on-hips, I know something is amiss.

"What's wrong?" I say.

"Nothing's exactly wrong..." She pulls the top blanket down an inch or so from underneath my father's chin, folds it over so that his chest is fully covered but his neck is exposed and free. "It's just that, although it might not seem so sometimes to you or me, people with your father's disease crave reassurance through habit, routine. Even people whose disease is as advanced as your father's. It makes them feel more settled, somehow."

"Right. So what can we do? What can I do?"

"Well, it's just that your uncle used to read to him before he went to sleep."

"*My* uncle? My Uncle *Donny*?"

"Every night that I can remember since your father's been with us."

My Uncle Donny who skims the back of breakfast cereal boxes to get to the good parts. The same man who, when he saw me reading once in a lawn chair in the backyard as a teenager, asked me how I could do *that* when it was so nice outside I could be doing *anything*?

"What does he read him?" I say.

"I don't know what you'd call them, but those slips of paper you can get at the convenience store or at the grocery store with all the hockey games listed on them that you can bet on. He'd read those."

"Betting slips? Pro-Line betting slips?"

"I don't know their name, but the government one, the one that says who's playing who and how much you can win."

Pro-Line betting slips. Montreal at Boston, the Bruins paying one and a half at home, the road team paying out two and a quarter, who sounds like the best bet? Christ. I don't know whether I should be angry or appreciative. Christ.

* * *

"WHAT DO YOU CALL IT WHEN PEOPLE cut themselves? On purpose, I mean."

Rachel lifts her head off my chest; lies on her side, head resting in her hand. "I guess it was as good for you as it was for me."

"No complaints here, believe me," I say, sliding my hand underneath the sheet and placing it on her naked back. Rachel's sheets are white Egyptian cotton and 1000 thread count, almost as soft as her skin.

"Do you own a dog?" she says.

"Why?"

"Do you?"

"I used to. Why?"

"You just patted me. And it's not the first time, either."

"I didn't pat you." I almost say *I caressed you*, but that doesn't sound right either, sounds too intimate, like something a long-time lover might do. "I stroked you."

"Whatever you say," she says, getting up from the bed, sheet wrapped around her like a toga. "Just don't expect me to fetch your pipe and slippers."

Except for in bed—and once on the rug—I've yet to see Rachel naked. You would have thought she'd want to show off her new and improved body every opportunity she got. It's crossed my mind to ask her what it feels like to look like—to *be*—someone else, but I figure it's really none of my business. If she wanted to talk about it, she'd talk about it.

"Cutters," she calls through the closed bathroom door.

"What?"

"You asked me what people who injure themselves are called. Cutters. Although I think self-mutilators is the preferred expression."

The toilet flushes, and Rachel, wearing a thick white cotton housecoat, emerges from the bathroom. She takes the remote off one of the side tables and clicks on the television. There's a TV in nearly every room of her apartment.

"I'll just be in and out," I say, sliding out of bed and heading for the shower.

"Why bother then?"

I stop at the bathroom door. "What do you mean?"

She hesitates. "Nothing," she says. "Take your shower." Rachel sits on the end of the bed, right leg crossed over left, the remote control in her hand, flipping channels.

"If it's a problem for me to use the shower, I won't."

"I didn't say that."

"No, but…"

"But no I didn't. So shower already."

I'm considering putting at least my underwear on and finding out what she's obviously upset about when she saves me the trouble of looking for them.

"It's just that, it's as if you can't stand to smell like me for five minutes after we've had sex."

"*That's* why you're angry?"

Rachel finally finds something worth leaving on—a reality show I can only presume—five sulky twenty-some-things slouching around an enormous glass table and all yelling at each other at the same time.

"I told you," I say. "I like to shower when I'm here only because I don't want to dirty the bathroom at home any more than I have to, because of the people coming over to look at the house. Laura says a dirty bathroom can be a real deal breaker."

"Oh, well, if *Laura* says it."

"What's that mean?"

"Nothing. Except that apparently Laura Mackenzie is still running my life."

"In what possible..." I interrupt my question because I realize I don't want Rachel to answer it. She's beautiful and happy now—as happy as anybody else, anyway—and Laura isn't. What else could she want? I realize I don't want to know the answer to that question either. "Look, this is just about trying to keep a clean bathroom, all right? That's all."

"If you say so."

"That's the only reason."

"Okay."

"Really."

"*Okay*." She shows she's serious about ending the argument by looking at me and away from the TV, although without switching it off or even turning the sound down. One of the girls on the program shouts, "I drownded it because it

153

wouldn't stop going off!" and the others laugh and whoop and bang on the table. I'd been in enough spats with Sara to know that arguing etiquette dictates that I go to Rachel and hug her to help put this misunderstanding officially behind us, but I stay where I am, in the doorway to the bathroom.

"So why do you think people do it?" I say. "The cutters, I mean."

"Why the sudden interest in self-mutilation? Do you have something you want to tell me?"

"I think a friend might be one. Maybe. I'm not sure."

"A friend."

"Sort of a friend, yeah."

"If you don't want to tell me, that's fine."

"Thanks."

"Totally fine."

"Thanks."

Rachel looks back to the television. "Can you please go take your shower now?"

*   *   *

I WORKED ALL DAY AND THE WORK went well—put down nearly five hundred words in fact, many of which I'm optimistic will survive tomorrow afternoon's revising scything. When the words do what you tell them to and occasionally—miraculously—tell you things you didn't even know you knew, there's very little temptation to check your e-mails or troll for records on eBay or Google the soft drink Wink, your dad's preferred gin mix, just so you can find out once and for all what year they stopped making it. And when the laptop is shut tight and that day's word total tallied, the delightful illogicality of feeling exhaustingly empty and yet, somehow, simultaneously brimming bursting. Then: a hot shower, a cold beer, and the rest of the day or night wide open and earned. Lucky days like these, I almost forget that the best part of it is over, that Barney isn't going to be whimpering at the front door later on because Sara is home from work and on the porch fishing for her keys in her bag and that we aren't going to phone in our usual takeout order to the Vietnamese place around the corner and pick it up on our way home from taking Barney for his evening walk with a quick stop at the Film Buff to select that night's DVD. And even if they were out of pan-fried noodles and forgot to substitute tofu for shrimp in the mixed vegetables again and the movie was a howling farce that unfortunately was advertised as a serious drama and the dog decided he needed to go outside for a pee five minutes after the lights had been turned off and tomorrow morning's alarm had been set, it was still going to be Sara and Barney and me. The world might have been skulking around outside, but we were our own world all together inside, and how could it ever be otherwise?

The only thing that got in the way of getting done what had to get done today was when, taking a break an hour or so in—popping a fresh can of Mountain Dew, kneading the small of my back while staring out the front window—I felt a sudden, unexpected sensation of excitement I couldn't account for. The same thing happens sometimes when a feeling of anxiety or anger invades your mind but you can't remember what you're supposed to be so upset about. That kind of amnesia is to be encouraged. This time, though, I took a sip and concentrated but still couldn't recollect what I was apparently supposed to be so pleased about; until, sitting back down at the kitchen table and my computer, it came to me: I was going to see Samantha tonight. I was going to see her after my work was done and I was going to tell her who died tonight, who I'd been writing about. I was also somehow going to get her to talk about those marks on her arms. It took me fifteen minutes online—during which I bid successfully on a rare promotional copy of David Bromberg's eponymous debut album—before my mind was back on Willie P. Bennett and why his music mattered and what both it and his life had to tell us. Later on, when my cell phone rang and Rachel's name came up on the caller I.D., I let it go to voice mail.

The pockmarked moon blushing high and bright and white and the doors of Buttercup Village locked and double-locked tight for the night are my cues to occupy the park bench and for Samantha to see me sitting there and to take her spot on the swing set. So I don't. Samantha's no Lolita and I'm definitely not some horny Humbert—which would be disgusting, but at least explicable—so what do I want with an eighteen year-old self-mutilating pothead? And I've got a girlfriend—sort of; a woman who I can spend time with, anyway, if spending time with a woman is what I want.

I manage half-an-hour's worth of garbage-bagging my mother's clothes for drop-off at the Salvation Army before the aroma of her favourite perfume, Downy fabric softener, spooks me out of my parents' bedroom. Leading to nearly forty-five minutes of filling cardboard box after cardboard box with my father's tools, each thump and clank an indifferent affront to every meticulously cleaned and carefully stowed object. Resulting in finally listening to Rachel's phone message, the gist of it being that if I wasn't doing anything tonight and didn't want to just sit around my parents' house feeling lonely, why didn't I call her back and she could pick me up and we could go to her place and have a drink and talk and just, well, whatever. I erase the message and open a bottle of red and grab my coat.

I sit and slug from the bottle and avoid looking at Samantha's house, not sure if it's because I do or don't want to see her come out of it. When I hear the familiar creak of her front door, however, I'm relieved, no confusion there. Which in itself is confusing enough. Thankfully I possess the necessary resources to blot my bewilderment, take a good long gulp of wine. She passes me in the dark and sits on a swing and strikes a match.

In the time it takes her to take her first toke, "So. Who died tonight?" she says.

First things first, duty before pleasure. "What did your guidance counsellor say when you told him you wanted to apply to U of T?"

"Didn't anyone ever tell you that it's considered rude to answer a question with another question?"

"You forget: I was born here. Rudeness is my birthright."

When I don't add anything else, appear content to tip my tipple and enjoy the free light show the stars in conjunction with the dark sky are putting on tonight, "I didn't tell him," she says. I knew she wouldn't lie to me; it would be easier for both of us if she did, but I knew she wouldn't.

"Why not? Time's running out. Maybe it already has."

I don't have to turn around to know she's shrugging her shoulders.

"Why not?" I repeat.

"I am," she says.

"'I am' what?"

"I am going to tell him."

"Okay. So why—"

"Just let me finish, all right?"

I pull from the bottle. "All right." As a gesture of good faith, I take an extra pull.

"I think I might want to go," she says. "I mean, if I go anywhere, I think that might be one of the places I want to go to. If you've got some sort of commission deal going with the U of T recruiting office, I'm sure your cheque is in the mail."

"But?"

"But"—she puffs, she ponders, "but I need to deal with something else first."

I know what *something else* is just as much as she knows that I know, but if we're going to talk about it, I can't be the one to bring it up, she'll have to be the one to raise the subject. I play dumb, not a particularly difficult role for me to pull off. "What, like your transcript or something like that? That's what he's there for. You worry about your grades, let him worry about that stuff."

"It's not my transcript."

"What is it then?"

"Something else."

"Yeah, I get that part. What is it?"

"Something."

"Something what?"

"Something personal, all right?"

I raise the bottle to my mouth; keep it there so I don't have to say anything. I stand up from the bench. "Hey, I not only got a nice eBay shipment of new vinyl in the mail today, I found a record player and a receiver and a pair of cheap speakers at a pawnshop that actually work. The needle's not great, but it does the job. What do you say we move this party inside?"

"Okay." She said it, but she doesn't get up.

"Sometime tonight, or—"

"I said okay," she says, finally rising.

She ends up a few steps ahead of me at my parents' front door. "It's not locked," I say.

Arms crossed, head down, "It's not my house. I don't go where I'm not invited."

"Christ, you really aren't from Chatham, are you?"

Inside, I don't look at her while she gets settled on the couch, don't want her to feel any more self-conscious than she already is. I stand at the kitchen table and sort through that morning's eBay delivery as if I'm alone. We're both waiting for her to say what we both know she's going to say.

"Who died tonight?" she says.

Without looking up from the stack of records, "Willie P. Bennett. Willie P. Bennett died tonight."

"I suppose I shouldn't be surprised by now that I haven't heard of him."

"Especially him. He wasn't only brilliant, he was Canadian. You can't get much more obscure than that."

I give her time to take out her joint and light it and pull off her hood, if not her coat. I spray a light mist of water and rubbing alcohol over side one of Karen Dalton's *In My Own Time*; begin to gently wipe it down counter-clockwise.

"Willie P. Bennett sang about coming down from Thessalon, how Toronto was not his home, but Toronto was where I saw him play for the first time, at the Free Times Café when I was in first year university, thirty people—tops—jammed into a room no bigger than this one, all of them knowing what they were in for except for me. All I knew about country-folk was through my Neil Young albums, and believe me, even that puny war was dearly paid for, no girl at CCI willing to find out if side two of *On the Beach*—the slow side, the one with just the title track, 'Motion Pictures,' and 'Ambulance Blues'—was a turn-it-up turn-on, no radio station out of Detroit disposed to extending their idea of heavy metal to a steel guitar bar."

"What's a steel guitar bar?"

"It's what you play a steel guitar with."

"But of course."

"Shall I continue or not?"

"I suppose."

"You suppose?"

"Just keep going."

I pause before resuming, pretending as if I actually have a choice. "One of the things I wanted to do when I left for university and Toronto was to go to an actual folk club and see an actual folk singer. I looked in *Now* magazine under the listing for Folk and picked the Free Times Café because it was near Spadina and College, two streets I at least knew the names of. I forget who I went with—it doesn't matter who I went with—I forget who I went with because what I do remember is that when I walked home that night back to my room in residence I had a song-buzzing brain and a self-financed, homemade cassette tape that Willie P. sold for ten dollars at the end of the show from a yellow cloth bag slung over his shoulder. It was self-financed and homemade because, I later learned, the three albums he recorded in the seventies were put out by a small Canadian label that no longer existed, and by the late-eighties, the darkest of the dark ages of popular music, anything un-synthesized and non-digitalized was sonically suspect, an age when otherwise intelligent people routinely referred to Madonna and Prince as geniuses and *Born in the USA* was considered roots music."

"Did this guy die too?"

"You do recall that every chapter of the book I'm writing begins with 'I was there the night he died.'"

"I know, but ... this one was in Toronto, you must have known him, right? Sort of?"

"People you know can die just as easily as those you don't."

"I've known people who've died."

"It's nothing to brag about."

"I know. But I have. I'm just saying."

I wait until she's relit her joint and I've finished removing any dust, smudges or human hair particles from side one of the Dalton album before flipping it over and starting all over again.

"Anyone who I thought deserved him, I dragged them off to see him—girlfriends and friends became ex-girlfriends and strangers, but the years couldn't touch the music, even Time, the biggest bully there is, can never touch the music. Good music, I mean. And even though a hundred dollar cut of the door was considered a very good night's take and it was usually only other musicians and freaks like me, who'd hunted down all of the out-of-print albums and traded bootlegs of folk festival shows, who knew who he was and what his music meant, songs like 'White Line' and 'Storm Clouds' and 'Down to the Water' and 'Lace and Pretty Flowers' are as good as any of the best stuff John Prine or Guy Clark or even Townes Van Zandt were writing back then. And just because no one knows it doesn't mean it's not true."

"I suppose all of those people are dead too."

I'm in the home stretch now, so don't answer, lift my bottle of wine instead.

"So here's what happens—here's what always happens—yet I'm always surprised and affronted and enraged each and every time it does, so who's really the real fool?" I answer my own question by taking another drink. "Two months after Willie P. Bennett died of a heart attack, age much-much-too-soon, some arts organization I thankfully can't remember the name of but whose members, no doubt, considered it a day of national mourning when the Royal Canadian Air Farce went off the air and who believe that an honest man in the White House is a sure cure for all that ails America, announced the inauguration of a new "Heritage Award" meant to honour an unjustly neglected album of Canadian roots music. And the winner is? *Lightfoot!* by Gordon Lightfoot." I raise my bottle—too quickly—and crack its lip against my two front teeth. "The man has a star on the sidewalk in front of Honest Fucking Ed's Seafood Restaurant, for Christ's sake."

Samantha offers me the joint and a tight-lipped, stillborn smile intended to keep her smoke from getting out and me from getting any more upset. I want neither mind-muddying pot nor gentle consolation, however; desire, instead, metaphysical justice and posthumous glory for Willie P. Bennett and every other songwriter or barber or bus driver who ever gave a shit only to discover that the world isn't particularly interested. Or, failing that, a couple fat lines of pharmaceutical quality cocaine and side one of *Trying to Start Out Clean* played just as loud as my crappy new second-hand stereo will allow. "Stay where you are," I say, placing Willie P.'s first album on the turntable and the needle in the groove to the first track while managing to sit back down on the couch just as the opening banjo lick that announces "Driftin' Snow" blows out of the speakers.

And blow it does, song one to song six—bluegrass torch songs impeccably strummed and sung without ever once losing that inspired looseness that's a necessary component of any art form aspiring to avoid the aesthetic sin of being goddamn arty. In the pause between 'Don't You Blame Your Blues On Me' and 'Country Squall,' "Complimentary novel-writing advice," I say. "Literariness is the enemy of literature."

"Do you expect me to write that down or something?"

The song's starting—there's no time to slap back her sarcasm with my own. "Just listen to 'Country Squall,'" I say. "It's only a little over two minutes long. Before you know it, it's over."

Chapter Ten

RACHEL HAS MADE ME PROMISE to get everyone I know to sign the latest petition, both online and on paper—which, now that apparently everyone who has the power to do something about it has signed off on CCI's closing, might be the last petition, this one a last-gasper going directly to the Provincial Minister of Education—so I'm at Steady Eddie's house, not counting Uncle Donny and a handful of others, the only other person left in Chatham I've known longer than the last four weeks. I want his signature, but what I need is his steadiness, that uniquely Eddie way of making the next laugh, the next beer, the next Red Wings game all that really matters, everything else just a little less important if not downright irrelevant. I could use some downright irrelevance.

"They weren't skating," I say. "And nobody was going to the net, not even Datsyuk. You can get away with that against a team like Columbus, but they better get their act together pretty soon, the playoffs are only a month away."

Eddie is less than his usual steady self tonight for some reason—reluctant snorts instead of real laughter, sipping at his beer as if he's actually tasting it—so I'm attempting

163

to prime the pump, get him going flowing being Steady Eddie so I can be myself and not have to do anything but sit here on his riding lawnmower and listen and laugh.

"I don't know," he says. "I didn't see the game. I was working nights last week."

Not that that has anything to do with it. When you're shooting the shit in Eddie's garage, the less you know about a given subject, the more you simply act as if you do. Eddie sips and I gulp and we both look around the garage in spite of there being a hockey game on the TV, even if it's only the Maple Leafs. The house is where Eddie and his family live—the decapitated dolls lying abandoned on the stairs, the white plastic laundry basket marooned in the middle of the kitchen floor, the workout machine in the basement that, like the one in my parents' basement, has sprouted coats and hats since its premature retirement—but the garage is Eddie's. It's the clubhouse he never had as a kid and it's Saturday night and we're supposed to be giddying it up, not acting like a couple of forty-something men with forty thousand things on our minds.

I point with my bottle at the television. "The Leafs manage to pull this one out, that'll be two in a row, they'll be planning the Stanley Cup parade down Yonge Street next week." It's an old joke, and making fun of the Leafs is about as fair as rearranging a blind man's furniture, but Eddie, like my father and me, gets almost as much pleasure out of the Leafs' unending ineptitude as he does the Wings' continued excellence. Everyone needs to hate something, and we hate the Leafs. Anyway, anything to get him talking, laughing, anything other than nothing.

Eddie manages a snort and a sip, stares up at the TV, shakes his head in apology. "Sorry, man," he says. "I had to yell at my kid this morning and I've felt like crap all day."

"One of your girls?" I know he's got two young daughters, but how young and what their names are is beyond our bi-yearly visits.

He smiles, the first time tonight. "My little princesses? I know everybody thinks their kids are perfect, man, but Charlotte and Josie, they've never given me a moment's worry, believe me, either one of them." Which I don't believe, but even if it is true, how much heartbreak can a four-year-old really generate? It's got to be his oldest son, new-daddy Gavin.

"Gavin, goddamnit, he's a good kid, he really is, you know that."

Having met him maybe three times in my life, I don't know any such thing, but I nod anyway. "Sure he is."

"But sometimes he just doesn't think. I mean, I *know* he knows what's right and wrong, but sometimes it's like he's working against himself, you know what I mean? And it makes me so mad because, like you said, he's a good kid, he *knows* what he should be doing."

"Well, kids make mistakes. We both did and we turned out all right."

Eddie finally lifts his bottle and swallows. "But now he's a kid with his own kid. And the mistakes he makes now don't just screw up his own life."

I don't have a comforting cliché for that one, so I do the only thing that has a chance of helping, go to the beer fridge and get two more Blue. Eddie takes his beer although he's only half done the one he's holding. We both lift our eyes to the television mounted on the garage wall. If Ottawa gets one more goal, they'll be right back in it, a third period Maple Leafs collapse a very real possibility. You find your hope wherever you find it.

165

During a commercial break for a clinic that not only performs laser hair removal surgery for men but also breast reductions—"It's called Gynecomastia, guys," the woman in the ad says, "and it's *not* your fault"—the door that connects the house to the garage slams open and one of Eddie's tiny pig-tailed daughters wails her way right past me and right into her father's arms. Eddie picks her up and asks her what's wrong, and whether or not he understands what "SheandthatwaysaidnottoMummysaidso" means more than I do, he nonetheless manages to immediately transform her relentless crying into a persistent sniffle and rubs away her tears with the sleeve of his shirt and even manages to tease a flickering smile at the corner of her mouth with some gibberish that makes about as much sense to me as his daughter's. Then Eddie grabs her by the feet and hangs her upside down and the little girl laughs just as loudly as she was crying three minutes before.

I smile, want them to know I'm fine with this father-daughter moment, to take as long as they need, but I don't need to worry: neither one of them even knows I'm there.

* * *

THE STARS HAVE MANAGED TO SHOW up again, if a little on the late side. Each day stays a little bit lighter a little bit longer. Such seasonal subtleties are lost on my neighbour directly across the street, however, who's switched on his powerful front porch light and shows no sign of doing anything but letting it blaze away right through until morning. The park is out of the question, obviously—the spotlight from across the street guarantees that—so I decide to get a load of laundry done while hauling Salvation Army-bound boxes upstairs.

166

I put a load of clothes in the washer and begin to fill the spare bedroom with boxes. Each time, before I return downstairs for more of Dad's tools and Mum's scented candles and my old track and field trophies, I go to the living room window to see if the lighthouse keeper at 5 Dahlia Avenue has finally packed it in for the night, only to be greeted by a blast of 200-watt sacrilege. Even a new-fangled subdivision can seem inscrutably alive if the night is dark enough, but I can see everything from my front window that's really there and everything else that isn't. I transfer the clothes from the washer to the dryer and wish I had some speed. When not enough is happening, making it happen quicker is the most effective way of fooling yourself that there is.

I've run out of boxes, so I lug this and that up the stairs. The large fan we used BCAC (Before Central Air-Conditioning) that would follow the family around from the dinner table to the living room and that I would crawl up close to and speak directly into to hear my voice magically transformed sci-fi spooky; my mother's *Sounds of Nature* CD, the closest she ever got to allowing the great big mess that is the great outdoors into our lives; my pair of fifteen pound dumbbells, ten biceps-plumping reps with which were a before-school necessity: all of it pushed into the corner of the spare bedroom to wait for the truck from the Salvation Army to haul them away.

The clothes are dry so I dump them into the laundry basket. Sara was always cold—the thermostat was never high enough in the winter, it was never hot enough for her in the summer—and it used to piss me off, that I'd be melting in August when she would always ask me before our evening dog walk if it was cold outside, did I think she needed a sweater.

I'm carrying the basket upstairs when the waft of gentle warmth that is the just-dried clothes nearly knocks me to my knees. If Sara was in the bedroom when I'd return from the basement with the laundry from the dryer, I'd dump the entire steaming basket on her, a hot mud slide of freshly clean clothes. She'd roll around on the bed underneath the warm laundry like Barney would on his back on the couch after a particularly satisfying dinner.

Before I put the clothes away I go to the front window. That sonofabitch. When is he going to shut that goddamn light off? Doesn't he know that the night belongs to everyone?

* * *

"HOW ABOUT A MOVIE?" RACHEL SAYS.

"They're all terrible."

"You don't even know what's playing."

"I don't need to," I say. "They're either light romantic comedies or Us versus Them action movies or sub-Tolkien teenage escape-fests, with a token Highbrow Harlequin thrown in to make the dentists' wives and all of the other local intellectuals feel superior to everyone else in town because they go to see *films* and not mere *movies*."

"Jesus."

"What?"

"Nothing."

"No—what?"

"Let's rent a DVD then," Rachel says. "You can pick it out and make sure we don't watch the wrong thing and damn our souls for eternity."

"No thanks. There's only Blockbuster, and they just offer take-home versions of the same crap as what the theatres serve up."

We've had dinner, we've had sex, we're sitting side-by-side on the couch in Rachel's small living room. What I really want to do is go home and pound down a Mountain Dew or two and get properly jittery and get back to work on my book.

Don't misunderstand: I'm not disciplined, I just like to write. Sara used to call me the world's laziest workaholic. Just contemplating cutting the grass or talking to a neighbour about how long the sidewalk construction is taking overwhelms me with actual somatic weariness, a heaviness of head and heart that's as certain to result as a loss of light is when a cloud passes across the sun. But three or four hours of applying carefully considered black squiggles to an enemy white page has the entirely opposite effect—simultaneously repositions both feet on the earth and pushes my spirit to places it can't get to when, say, you're trying to figure out how to hang the new blind in the kitchen.

"Okay," Rachel says, standing up and clapping her hands once, loudly. "What if I open a bottle of wine and you help me with the letter I've got to get to the government by next week? I should have thought of this before. Who better to argue for CCI's continuing relevance than one of its most famous alumni?"

"I'm not famous."

"Compared to most everyone else you went to school with you are."

"That doesn't make me famous. That just means I'm not anonymous."

We both look at the TV, which is never not on at Rachel's. Over footage of several red mini-skirted dancing bears performing before thousands of happily applauding children and their circus-going parents, a sombre British voice explains exactly how bears are taught to "dance:" how music is played while the metal floor underneath them is heated enough to burn their feet, compelling them to hop from foot to foot, thereby guaranteeing that when the same music is played again later they instinctively hop about, hoping to avoid the remembered pain.

"My God, that's terrible," Rachel says, sitting back down. "I had no idea."

"I've got to write this down," I say, pulling the pen and notepad out of my pocket.

"Why would you want to write something like that down?"

"So I won't forget it."

"It's terrible. It's worse than terrible."

"I know. And it's a terribly powerful metaphor, too."

"A metaphor for what?"

"I don't know yet. I'll know when I find it. And when I do, I don't want to forget."

Rachel looks back at the TV and I scribble in my notepad. She gets up again, but this time without clapping her hands.

"Where are you going?" I say.

"I'm getting my keys. I'm going to drive you home."

"Are you mad at me?"

"No," she says, going into the bedroom.

And I don't think she is, either.

* * *

FINALLY, SOME GOOD NEWS. Great news. News so great I wish I had someone to tell it to.

The couple who came by last week have made an offer on the house—less than what we're asking for, but more than enough money to make me credit card debt-free again and to lay a nice fat nest egg in Dad's bank account. I consider calling Rachel—pick up the phone and enter the first three numbers, in fact—but how can I be yakky happy when Samantha is on the other side of the street so obviously sullen sad? I'm not my teenage neighbour's keeper, but as soon as the house is sold it'll be time to start thinking about going home. It's not the same now, it'll never be the same, but Toronto is home, at least I have a home to go back to. Samantha needs a home. Even if it's just for four forgettable undergraduate years. A home for now, anyway, a home along the way.

I know she'll show up if I do, but what I'll say once she does I'm a lot less sure of. Half a bottle of red wine later, I'm two for two: here she comes, and what the hell am I supposed to say to her? Whether because of the wine or the news of the offer on the house or because I'm simply tired of waiting for her to make the first confessional move, I hear myself ask, "So why do you see a psychiatrist?"

"So who died tonight?"

"You go first."

I can hear her slowly rocking on the swing set behind me, the dry grinding creak of the freezing chains every time she sways forward then backward. "I told you. It's my parents' idea."

"You mean your dad's?"

The creaking stops; I hear her flick her lighter once, twice, the third time getting the job done. "Yeah. His."

"Where's your mum in all of this? If you don't mind me asking."

"She's dead in all of this."

"I'm sorry to hear that."

"I thought you said you didn't like it when people said they were sorry your wife died?"

171

I pull from my bottle of wine. "I guess when the shoe is on the other foot it's easier to understand what the other person is feeling."

"I guess it is."

The swing set is creaking again. I take this as my cue to continue. "So it's just your brother and your dad and you."

"The last time I checked."

"So why did you say your parents make you see a psychiatrist?"

She's either thinking or toking or maybe both. Probably both.

"Habit, I guess," she says.

I know what she means. "I know what you mean."

"You do?"

My head says, *Shut up*, but my gut argues otherwise, argues that if you want this girl to tell the truth, you've got to give her back at least a little bit of the same.

"My wife Sara and I used to talk about everything. It used to feel like something wasn't real unless we discussed it. I remember coming home from her funeral and wanting to tell her about it, to go over what happened with her."

"That makes sense."

"It does?"

"After my mum died—I was fourteen—I used to get so disappointed that the sandwich in my lunch wasn't the peanut butter and banana on twelve grain bread that my mum always made."

"Who made your sandwiches after that?"

"My dad."

"You could have asked him to make them."

"It wouldn't have been the same." She takes a toke; I can almost hear her forcing the pot deep inside her lungs. "I don't know how she did it, but the way she

172

made them was so good, and every time, too. She had her own way of doing it. Nobody else can make them like my mum did."

"Sara used to wake me up if I was having a nightmare." I can't believe I just said that. I lift my bottle and see that it's almost empty and start to believe it a little bit more. "Once, I had a dream she was leaving me for some other guy and I guess I was screaming in my sleep and she woke me up. She was the reason I was screaming and she was the one who stopped me." I get up from the bench and go and sit on the swing next to Samantha's and take the joint from between her fingers. "Now when I have a nightmare I have to see it through to the end."

"Do you ever ... I mean, do you ever have nightmares about what happened? To her, I mean."

"Sometimes. Less than I used to."

"That's terrible." She takes the joint back.

"It has its advantages, actually. I'm usually really mad when it happens—sometimes at her, most of the time just at the fact it happened—and it lets me *be* mad, to really let go and rant and rave until I wake myself up."

"That's an advantage?"

"It means I don't have to be angry when I'm awake." This time she doesn't wait for me to retrieve the joint, hands it to me as soon as she's done. "You need to be angry—I'll probably always be angry—but I don't want to live that way. No one ought to live that way."

A woman bundled up in her scarf so tightly and with her toque tugged down so low and encased in a coat so big she almost isn't there scurries past us, her chihuahua as eager as she is to get where they need to go. I miss walking Barney, miss the easy virtue of doing a dog a favour. If we were in Toronto, the dog would be wearing a coat and boots likely worth as much as its owner's. Despite this, I miss Toronto too.

"Back in Oakville," Samantha says, "some of my friends and I used to have bulimia parties."

"That can't possibly be what it sounds like."

"It was totally stupid. I was the only one who ended up going through with it. Everyone talked so big about how we were all going to drink lots of water and we were all going to do it—no backing out—but when it came time to start, I was the only one to even go into the bathroom. And when I came back out everyone was looking at me like I was some kind of freak. What total wanksters." She tugs the hood of her sweatshirt forward on each side, flicks the roach onto the snow and sticks her bare hands into the pockets of her coat.

"That's one way of looking at it, I guess," I say.

"What do you mean?"

"I mean, maybe deciding not to force yourself to throw up isn't the worse decision a person can make."

"You don't get it. We made a pact. It was supposed to be a promise between friends. You know, BFF, all that crap."

"Maybe with friends like that…"

She grabs her phone from the pouch of her hoodie and makes herself invisible with her thumbs. I don't know who she could be texting, she's never mentioned any friends or a boyfriend, but I don't want to lose her to technology. I'll give her what she wants, but I'll give it to her my way, the life of a poet with a guitar, but with a message from me delivered directly to her.

"Townes Van Zandt died tonight," I say.

Samantha looks up from her phone. It's a start.

"Townes Van Zandt was a beautiful human being from the years 1968, the year of his first album, until 1978, the year of his last really good one. A mostly absentee father and quite often a nasty drunk and a dispenser of sweet and sour love depending on which way the wind blew, when he played his guitar and sang his songs, though, he was beautiful, he was perfect."

"Sounds like someone has got a pretty bad man crush."

Cynicism is preferable to sulking, so I keep going.

"He was like everybody—had advantages like being born rich, and disadvantages like being born rich and suffering from depression and undergoing electroshock therapy that left him with virtually no memory of the first ten years of life. But the thing, the main thing, is that your life and my life might be different from his, but it's still the same high, low, and in between, the same as it is for everyone all of the time everywhere."

I lift the wine bottle, but it's got nothing left to give. I'm on my own.

"The music he made came from what Texas does best, glopping together all of the good stuff from folk and country and blues and with a generous peppery dash of good old, old America weirdness. I said once in a book I wrote that when so-and-so sang, he made a broken heart seem like an attractive option. I say it again now."

"Okay," Samantha says. "But where's the but?"

"What *but*?"

"There's always a *but* to your stories."

"That's what makes them real."

"Because they really happened, you mean."

"No, because they're really real."

Samantha replaces her phone with her bag of weed, and I allow her a moment to roll another number. She takes the time to look at the snow that's started to fall instead. I look at it too.

"But he hurt himself. With booze, mostly, although it's not just what you put inside yourself that can hurt you. And for someone who believed that a good song was rarer and more important than anything else in the world, worst of all was that he ended up hurting his music, went from being a deft finger-picker with hands like delicate spiders to a lackluster strummer, and his voice, which was once fragile but forceful, became whispery and croaky weak. I know that the songs he wrote and the shows he played during those ten teeming years are better and will last longer than anything I'll ever do, and what right have I got to toss pebbles at the sun, but it's sad to watch beautiful things turn ugly, is all. It's just really sad."

It's still snowing. It looks like it might snow all night.

*   *   *

"SAM, I *STRONGLY SUGGEST* YOU reconsider your decision."

"Like I said, I just think we can do better."

"And like I said, this is a very weak market right now, and I'm personally very comfortable with their counter offer."

"That's less than what we wanted."

"By only ten thousand."

"Laura, I'm selling this house to help my father. It wouldn't feel right if I didn't get him everything I can."

"Well, as it stands right now, you're not going to be getting him anything."

I put the phone to my other ear.

"Look, Laura, I respect your professional opinion and I appreciate all the hard work you've put into this, but I'm going to have to say no, that's my final answer. Let's just keep showing the house and I'm sure we'll get our asking price soon enough."

"*Keep* showing the house? Sam, only one prospective buyer has come to see it. And they're the ones who made the offer."

"And I'm sure there'll be others."

The phone is silent. I switch it back to my other ear.

"If it's relevant to the sale of the house, do you mind if I ask you a personal question, Sam?"

"Shoot."

"Does this have anything to do with Rachel?"

"No. Why would it have anything to do with Rachel?"

"Well, I know you two have been seeing a fair bit of each other socially, and I wonder if maybe you might be delaying the sale of your parents' house so you'll have a reason to stay around Chatham a little longer."

"Laura, I can honestly say I haven't given Rachel a single thought through any of this."

"Okay, but if—"

"Honestly, I haven't considered her at all."

"Okay."

After I hang up, it occurs to me that I don't want to sound as indifferent to Rachel as I did, that I don't like how cold I came across. I hear the postman on the step and open the door in time for him to hand me my most recent eBay purchase, a pizza box-sized brown package with three new records inside, including a white label promotional copy of Gene Clark's *Two Sides to Every Story*. I can't wait to show it to Samantha. I'm sure she's never seen anything like it.

CHAPTER ELEVEN

I'VE MADE MY FIRST MINIMUM payment toward my Visa bill. Sara and I had a policy that plastic was strictly for emergency purchases. This month's minimum payment alone is almost as large as any total balance that we'd ever incurred. I hate to give money away to a credit card company, but I don't have any choice. All Laura needs to know is that I'm not accepting the offer we received because I'm holding out for a better one, but the real reason I'm in debt is because Samantha needs to hear who died, Samantha needs to hear the stories I've got to tell.

Stories that I'm uncomfortably way ahead of schedule in writing, incidentally. I didn't intend to be this far along in finishing *Lives of the Poets (with Guitars)*, it just happened. In a way, it's Samantha's fault that I'm almost done with what I don't want to be done with. I'd planned to stretch this project out until I was ready to write my next novel, a book that somehow has to incorporate Sara's death. It doesn't have to be about her, she doesn't even have to appear in it, but what happened to her and what it means to me has to find its way into words. You can choose where your book is set and who's in it and what they do and don't do, but you can't control what your book is about. My next novel could chronicle the uproarious cross-country adventures of Canada's reigning one-armed lawn bowling champion and his trusty monkey butler sidekick, but its guts would be about what it means to love someone and to lose someone and to have to go on living anyway. Problem is, once those guts get transplanted onto the page, that's where they'll do the majority of their living.

But Samantha needs these stories. In lieu of getting her to actually tell me why she cuts herself, I went on-line last week to try to understand why people in general do it. Everybody's bad news has its own inimitable tang, but apparently there are some things that are across-the-board bona fide for people suffering from her disorder. Like that cutting is basically a coping mechanism for stress, of which Samantha—with no mum, with a drunk for a dad, with a new school and town to adjust to, with university looming—clearly has. Like that the endorphins that the body releases when cut or injured feel good, and that people can actually become addicted to them when they're otherwise feeling emotionally bad. That some people cut themselves for an entirely different reason, to feel pain in order to feel more alive when they're prone to ordinarily feeling numb. That marijuana is a common form of self-medication since it tends to blunt the desire to self-mutilate.

Samantha needs these stories. I need to write them—would have written them anyway—but she needs to hear them. I need to write them now so I'll know what to say when I see her. She needs to know who died tonight. Who and how and what for.

I realize, of course, that this all sounds incredibly vain. Not that that's any surprise. I do, after all, tell stories for a living.

* * *

EVEN THOUGH I'M NOT GOING anywhere for awhile, I still need to finish packing up my parents' stuff, so I'm at No Frills to get more boxes for the things I'm keeping and garbage bags for what I'm either throwing out or donating to the Salvation Army. While I'm here, I decide to pick up a few non-packing-related items, but get stalled in the bakery section, the kamut bread that Sara insisted we eat and that I'd ordinarily buy from the health food store down the street not a Chatham grocery store staple. My flesh started to fill out around the same time that hers started to fall, and every aging step of the way Sara would add or subtract whatever was necessary for our continued good and happy health. We used to joke how at least we weren't going to have to endure the encroaching Hospital Years alone, and that if I could put up with her going completely grey, she was willing to accept me wearing my pants chest-high.

Once I settle on a loaf of rye bread whose primary ingredient isn't rye but wheat, I head for the dairy aisle, where I spot Rachel standing in front of a refrigerated wall of egg cartons. I watch her select one, open it up, and inspect it. She's obviously just finished work, still has her teaching clothes on—matching blue blouse and skirt, simple silver necklace, sensible heels—but looks...weary more than simply tired. The dozen eggs in her hand make the grade and get placed in her shopping cart.

I duck back into the pop and chips aisle and ditch the bread on a half empty pretzel shelf and magnet toward the store's exit. Once I'm outside, I can't understand why I'm there. Walking home, all I can come up with is that it felt like I saw something I shouldn't have.

*　*　*

I FEEL IT BEFORE I THINK IT, always an encouraging sign when the feeling is a good one. This one is a good one. My only concern is that the nurse who must have turned on the TV to the hockey game for my dad might have put it on a little too loud for some of the other, more sentient patients who might become agitated by it, I can hear it halfway down the hallway. I remember it's Saturday night, Hockey Night in Canada, hockey still hockey even if it's Maple Leafs hockey. Maybe they're getting thumped.

He sees me before I see him, springs up from the chair beside Dad's bed as soon as he spots me coming through the door. His arms are hanging at his sides like a long distance runner ready to race. Uncle Donny might be unforgivably selfish, but he's not stupid. At least not when it comes to his own self-preservation. He's probably expecting me to shout, so I don't.

"Where's the smart money tonight?" I say. "Whoever's playing the Leafs is probably your best bet."

"I haven't made a wager in over a month. I go to Gamblers' Anonymous meetings twice every week."

Uncle Donny viewed with suspicion any group or gathering larger or more organized than Christmas or Thanksgiving dinner with my parents and me, even tended to distrust his own union, used to complain how the big shots upstairs in the suits used to be decent guys when they were down on the line like everybody else, and that they had to be watched every minute now that they had their fingers on the purse strings. I have great difficulty imagining him standing up in some church basement full of strangers and announcing, "My name is Donny Samson and I'm a compulsive gambler."

"And I never bet against the Leafs." He says it like I'm supposed to be impressed.

"Well, that helps explain why you lost so much money, anyway."

"I never once bet against my own team."

"Congratulations. If you couldn't be loyal to your brother, at least you were a rock when it came to supporting the league's sorriest franchise."

I look at Dad for the first time since I came in the room. If you didn't know what was wrong with him, you might think he was just another guy killing just another Saturday night watching the game, pleasantly bored while waiting for a goal or a fight or something to liven up his night, his life. Uncle Donny sees what I'm looking at.

"He knows when it's hockey, you know," he says.

"Don't make me any more upset than I already am."

He contemplates keeping his mouth shut; looks at the TV, then back at me. He licks his lips. "I don't care what you say—or what any doctor says either—I know he's the happiest he is when the two of us are watching the game."

"The two of you."

"That's right."

"I can't believe I'm asking this, but do you mind enlightening me how you happen to know this to be true?"

Uncle Donny studies Dad's face for a moment. "I don't know. I just know it is. I just know it's true."

Not only is he now an enthusiastic exponent of group therapy, he's also a mystical seer of others' ineffable states. This from the same man whose favourite game with me when I was a kid was to get me to follow his "one skin" with my own "two skin" succeeded by his "three skin" before concluding with the inevitable "four skin."

"Yeah, well…" I say and pick up the remote from the side table and click off the television to prove my point.

There aren't any visitors tonight except for Uncle Donny and me. The only sound now that the game is off is Mr. Goldsworthy in the bed across the room making a low, repetitive, monotone noise with his mouth closed that to someone who didn't know any better might sound like humming.

I look at the clock on the far wall. "The game was almost over anyway," I say.

"I didn't say it wasn't," Uncle Donny says.

* * *

THE SUN, THE STILL INDUSTRIOUS SUN, has done its daily thing, come and gone and given way to a black sky stuffed full of bright white stars. The ratio is right. One living lifegiver is worth a billion dead suns, no matter how brightly they once shone upon a time. But some things are easier to do or say in the dark, so we need nighttime too. I'd waited for this evening's appearance while revising what I'd written over the last week, a chapter of *Lives of the Poets (with Guitars)* double dutying as a life lesson for Samantha. Art can't be didactic, but its manufacturers sure can.

I don't have to wait long on the park bench before I see her leave her house and cross the road and walk past me to the swing set. I give her time to take out her stash and light up and ask me who died. Instead, "Do you want some of this?" she asks.

I lift my bottle of wine without turning around on the bench.

"You know," she says, "in certain cultures, it's considered insulting to turn down the offer of a communal toke."

"What cultures?"

I hear her inhale, hard. "It's a big world. There've got to be some."

184

I lift my bottle to my lips without swallowing, not wanting to appear a party pooper, but also not wanting to turn tonight into a party where I'm too pooped to say what I want Samantha to hear. I'd primed the oratorical pump with a few glasses of red wine before I left home, and I've got to be careful not to flood the engine.

"Whatever," she says. "If you want to be an alky, it's your life."

I want to answer back that I'm not an alky—at least not an alky like her father is, the one who's clearly scared her clear of alcohol—but I also want her to remain unawares and stay open to what I've written, so I take the seat next to her on the swing set and offer a peace sign that she completes by slipping the joint between my two fingers.

"Don't do it for me," she says.

"I'm not. It's something you should know about me. I pride myself on my cultural sensitivity."

I puff and pass it back and hope I've got enough brain cells to spare so that my head can handle being pleasantly muddled when I also need it to be serious and sharp.

"Gram Parsons," she says. "Didn't he die tonight?"

In spite of being impressed, or at least surprised, that she knows who he is, "I don't do cover versions," I say.

"It's a request."

"I don't do requests."

"You wrote a novel about him, though, didn't you?"

Now I really am both impressed and surprised. "Something like that. Did you read it?"

She takes another hit, passes me the joint. "I read *about* it. On your website."

"Gee, I'm flattered. The whole website, or just selected parts?"

"Didn't you know that my generation has a tragically short attention span because of all the video games we play and the music videos we watch?"

"And my generation believed that if you didn't eat beef and drink two glasses of homogenized milk with every meal you risked getting sick, and that asbestos was the insulation of the future. That didn't stop us from reading a book without pictures now and then."

"I believe they're called graphic novels, Grandpa."

"We read comics too. We just felt guilty about it if we were still reading them when we were old enough to vote."

And then I don't feel so smart anymore; feel a-okay with it, too, which is even worse, like if I just sit here gently rocking in this icy nighttime breeze long enough everything will take care of itself in time, quintessential stoner satori. This is the price of the happiness that pot begets. I'm okay, you're okay, let's microwave a frozen pizza.

"Do you ever see birds?"

I think that's what she says. "Did you just say, 'Do you ever see birds?'"

"Yeah, I mean ... I mean, I know there are birds, obviously, but ... Do you ever *see* them? I don't think I ever remember seeing any. Not lately, I mean."

I've got to act fast before I lose her.

"Janis Joplin died tonight," I say.

"But I didn't ask you who died."

"It doesn't matter. I'm telling you. Janis Joplin died tonight."

"But it doesn't work that way."

"It does tonight. Tonight, I'm telling you, Janis Joplin died."

Before she can again object to my willful disregard of our unspoken *tête-à-tête* etiquette, I proceed to tell

Samantha all about Janis Joplin. About how she was an overweight, acne-scarred high-school outcast from Port Arthur, Texas in the late 1950s—where and when being a high-school outcast was the real geeking deal—and how, just like the song says, her life was saved by rock and roll, except it wasn't rock and roll, but Bessie Smith and Leadbelly and Odetta and Big Mama Thorton records. How like thousands of other kids, she eventually migrated to San Francisco in the hope of fewer hometown hassles and more funky freedoms and how she found what she was looking for in a five-man blues-rock band that she stood in front of and which took their orders and inspiration from her because she was the actual reason everyone came out to listen—real rock and roll feminism. I tell Samantha how she screwed who she wanted to screw—men and women both, it didn't matter which, just as long as they were either attractive or interesting or, ideally, both. How she sang how she wanted to sing—ear-drum-bursting, heartache-healing, soul-stirring screams and whispers and sighing supplications. I tell Samantha how she might have worn feathers in her hair and kaleidoscope-coloured bell-bottoms, but she was still that same pimply plump high-school freak from Port Arthur, Texas, the one who forced the world to shut its big mouth and listen to what she had to say because, clearly, it didn't have the balls necessary to speak for itself. I tell Samantha how—and this is the part I've been building toward, this is what tonight is all about—everyone at one time or another drinks or smokes or sniffs or loves too much, but here's the thing, here's the thing to never forget: heroin is no win, and Janis knew it and did it again and again anyway, and she lost. She knew she had a problem, she knew she had a reason to live, and yet she died on a hotel room floor with the change for the cigarette machine still clenched in her right hand, she'd barely even tied-off before she hit the carpet.

"Asshole."

"That's not how to look at it," I say. "The way to look at it is she needed help—more help than she was getting. That's the point."

"Not *her*, you asshole," Samantha says, standing up from the swing. "What an asshole *you*."

I stand up as well; point at myself just to make sure there's no further confusion as to who she's referring to. "Me?"

"Is this what you wanted to see?" she says, ripping off her coat and slamming it over her shoulder to the ground like an overmatched wrestling opponent.

I pat down the air with open palms. "Let's try to keep it down, okay?"

Next to go is her perennial blue hoodie, but this time not south, but at me, the zipper catching me in the right eye. Both of my eyes shut tight of their own volition, and the right one begins to water.

"Look at me."

"Jesus Christ, I can't look at you, you've fucking blinded me."

"I said look at me. This is what you wanted to see, so look at me."

The injured eye won't cooperate—is too busy sending salty water down the right side of my face—but the left one is game. What it sees is Samantha in her white sports bra with both arms extended in front of me for inspection, old flesh-coloured scars alternating with fresh red welts up and down each forearm. Lucky there are so many stars out tonight or I wouldn't be able to see them so well. Lucky.

"I just wanted to help," I say, trying not to stare at the mess of her flesh. "I *do* want to help."

"With your bullshit stories with their stupid moral lessons? You really think a *story* is going to make me stop cutting myself? My God, you are *so* vain. You come across like you're so laid back and above all the bullshit, but you're just as full of yourself as everyone else. Is that what you've been doing every time you told me about someone who died? God, I can't believe I sat there like some kind of little groupie and listened to you."

"No, no, that wasn't what happened at all. Before, it was just us talking, I swear. Because I liked talking to you. I *do* like talking to you. Tonight was the first time I ... Look, I was little drunk, maybe I came across a little ... pedagogical, but the point is still ... "

Samantha gathers up her clothes from the frozen ground and walks away without bothering to put them back on. Her naked shoulder blades look like amputated wings. You'd think she would hurry home—me still standing there, the cold air, someone who might see her—but if you did, you would be wrong.

CHAPTER TWELVE

I'M EIGHTEEN AGAIN, AND TIME travel isn't all it's cracked up to be.

It's almost midnight on Friday night and Steady Eddie is behind the wheel and the radio is on and we've each got a can of beer between our thighs and there's nowhere we have to be, we're just driving around, but it's a single Coors Light Tall Boy each because drinking and driving drunk is a grown-up no-no and the radio is one long commercial only occasionally interrupted by songs we've heard a million and twelve times before and never need to hear again and we're not in Eddie's dad's 1980 Chrysler Le Baron coupe but in the Steady One's brand new GMC Sierra HD with a 360 horsepower Vortec Six Litre V8, six-speed automatic transmission, and towing and payload capacity far superior to his last truck, features and luxuries he neither needs nor can afford. But he just got the good news that he's staying on at the factory, at least through the spring and the summer, so what better way to celebrate being able to scrape by for a few more months than by adding a truck payment to his already fat stack of monthly bills? Money is for spending, after all, life is for living, you know, you only go around once, don't forget.

"Remember the Capitol Theatre?" Eddie says, hand on the wheel, pointing with his pinkie.

"Sure." Someone's parents would drop you off, someone else's would pick everyone up out front, two dollars to get in and a dollar for popcorn or a chocolate bar and a pop and teenage ushers with flashlights and "O Canada" before the movie. I'm sure I wasn't the only Chatham adolescent to see his first pair of female breasts after bluffing his way into *Porky's* at the Capitol.

"The city bought it and are turning it into a real theatre—you know, for plays and stuff." Both the Capitol and the Centre closed down in the early nineties, near-century-old monuments to Chatham's downtown, boarded up and forgotten in favour of a conveniently located cement box that can show eight Tinsel Town chimeras at once.

"That's good," I say. "That's good for the city." Which it is, I suppose, even if an abandoned and darkened three-story Edwardian building has more tragic dignity than a refurbished community playhouse specializing in local productions of *Oklahoma!* and the inevitable Christmas *Nutcracker*. But the desolately sublime doesn't pay anybody's bills. And Sara, who grew up in Toronto, said her parents took her to the Nutcracker every year and she hated it until the year they didn't go, when she missed it so much she made them attend the following year and every year after that until she left home. So, good for the Capitol Theatre. Good for Chatham.

We've reached the end of King Street; Eddie flicks on his blinker. "Let's check out the old school," I say.

"You got it," Eddie says, just glad to have somewhere else to show off his gleaming new monster mobile. What's the point of having something if you can't use it to make other people jealous?

192

We take turns ducking our heads dash-level to take a sip from our beer, a pair of sensible rebels. "Hey how's that place, that Thames View, taking care of your old man? Pretty good, I bet. Mum's got an aunt in there and Mum says she's never been busier or had more friends."

"It's good," I say. "They take good care of him. But my dad, he's not … he's in a different part of the building. He's in the Alzheimer's ward, so … "

"Right, right." Eddie lowers his head and takes another sip, sorry, I can tell, for raising the topic. "Your uncle, he's got to be a big help over there, though. I mean, when you're in T.O., your dad has family there. That's important."

"My uncle's a prick," I say. "Don't ask me why, but he is."

Eddie raises a steady hand—international sign language for *Your family and the shit it gets up to is off limits, I understand*—and concentrates on the road. He's not only trying to be nice, he's also—goddamn it—right: my dad *does* need someone other than a paid professional to keep him company, even if he doesn't know whose company he's actually in. I realize at this very moment, sitting four feet off the ground in Eddie's truck, that I'm going to have to forgive Uncle Donny. Not forget—you don't have a choice about that— but forgive, at least enough to trust him again to be my point man in Chatham when I'm three hours away in Toronto. I'm pissed off, but also relieved. And surprised—astounded, actually—at how easy it is to change your mind about something you couldn't imagine changing your mind about.

"How's the sale of the house going, anyway? Anybody sniffing around yet?"

"Not many," I say. "One, actually."

"That's rough. Just wait, though, somebody'll make an offer, you'll see."

"Somebody already did."

"Oh yeah?"

"But it was under what I'm asking."

"Low-balling you, eh?"

"By ten thousand."

"Just ten?"

Eddie pulls the truck in front of CCI and puts it in park, lets it idle. I don't answer him, both because it's obvious what he thinks—thinks the same thing as my real-estate agent, that I should accept the offer—and because it's only twenty-two more days until the vampires at Visa are due their next currency feeding.

"Want to go for a walk?" I say.

"Where?" Even if you don't have a new thirty-five thousand dollar vehicle, walking in Chatham is what you do when you can't afford to drive.

"I don't know. Is the football field still there?"

"I guess so. My neighbour's kid is going out for Junior this spring, so they've still got a team."

"For now."

"For now."

We get out of the truck and walk past the school—dark and empty and somehow the same building we filled with our voices and footsteps and nervous daydreams as teenagers—on the way to the football field behind it. The stars and the moon are all the light we need to get us there.

"I hear you're dating Rachel Turnbal," Eddie says.

"Who told you that?"

"I don't know. I don't remember. Somebody."

It's a town of less than 40,000, Eddie has lived in it his entire life, as has nearly everyone else who calls it home: I believe him. "We're not dating," I say. "We're just spending some time together."

"Why aren't you?"

"Why aren't we what?"

"Dating."

"Look," I say. "The shed."

The shed was where all of the practice equipment was kept—the orange pylons for running agility drills, the shields for blocking practice, the sled for the linemen to work on their pushing and pulling. Junior football was in the spring, senior football in the fall. The offence and the defence took turns getting out the equipment, and in the first week of September, if you were the one with the key to the padlock, it was like opening the door to a wooden kiln. Tonight there are icicles hanging from the doorframe.

"She sure got hot all of a sudden," Eddie says.

"Who? Rachel, you mean?"

"Hell yes, Rachel. Like you didn't notice."

"I noticed. But she's still the same person she was in high-school."

"Oh yeah?"

"Yeah. She's nice. She's a nice person."

"Is that why she's not your girlfriend?"

"What do you mean?"

"Because she's nice?"

Today was mild most of the day, and the melted snow has changed forms, has attached itself to the gravel on the track around the football field like sparkly glaze on a dirt and pebble crumble cake. Without saying anything, Eddie and I start around the track. Every practice would begin with a sprint around both goalposts. It hardly seemed worth it, it was so easy and over with so quick. Eddie unzips his fly and waters one of the goalposts. I look around to see if it's clear and join him. Little boys can't help sneaking a peek at the wee-wee whizzing next to them; middle age men can't resist sizing up the gut—Bigger? Smaller? The same?—of the guy standing closest. Forty-four years later and still fretting over a couple of inches.

"Let's jog the rest of the way," I say.

"Are you nuts?"

"Come on. For old time's sake."

"Screw old time's sake. My running days are over."

I run on my own the rest of the way around the posts, stand panting in place back where I started. Eddie's laughing when he finally gets there.

"Man, you need a beer," he says. "You look like you just ran a marathon."

*   *   *

DAD HAS A FEVER AND SOME liquid in his lungs and abnormally high blood pressure. Nothing to worry about too much at the moment, the doctor says, but definitely something worth keeping an eye on. Alzheimer's patients don't die of Alzheimer's—the body eventually just packs it in after being beaten and battered so hard for so long. Stroke and pneumonia are two of the most common causes of death among patients in advanced stages. Stages don't get any more advanced than Dad's.

Uncle Donny was at Thames View when I got there, had gotten the same phone call that I had. The first thing I noticed wasn't Dad, who, fever and liquid in his lungs and raised blood pressure or not, looked the soporific same, but Uncle Donny, specifically the cell phone hanging in its cheap black plastic case from his belt. He saw me see it too, said, "After they called me about the fever, I picked it up at the 7-Eleven on the way over here. I don't want to be somewhere and then have them call me and me not know what's going on." He was holding ice chips to my father's lower lip to help ease the fever. I believed him.

When Dad's temperature dropped and visiting hours were over, we walked in silence to the parking lot without Uncle Donny offering to drive me home or me asking him to, but him doing just that anyway. I slipped one of his Rat Pack CDs into the car's disc player so that neither of us would have to say anything. Dean Martin serenaded us home with "That's Amore."

Once inside the house I decide to phone Rachel, to tell her we need to talk, but when I get her voicemail I say I'm just checking in, no big deal, no need to call back. There's nothing left to pack or to throw out or to donate— what little that's left is what I need to get by while I'm here—and I finished the second to last chapter of *Lives of the Poets (with Guitars)* last night, sound compositional practice dictating that I wait at least a couple of head-clearing days before beginning what will be the end of the first draft. What I want to do is what I'm afraid won't happen. If I take my usual spot on the park bench and Samantha doesn't show up, I feel as if I won't ever see her again.

I stand on the front porch, neither here nor there, pretending that's where I want to be. The night is starless and windy, but late-March almost-mild, you can smell the earth beneath the neighbourhood lawns beginning to wake up. I'm wearing gloves, but I don't need them, drop them to the porch and stick my hands inside my coat pockets. Samantha's front door opens and closes and I hear her crossing her lawn.

Except he isn't she. He is her father. Crossing my lawn at a steady clip and not, for a change, wobbling; walking straight and standing tall, in fact. And talking to me.

"I want you to stay away from my daughter."

"Pardon?" I say, although I understand him just fine, at least the words that he's using.

"You heard me. You're lucky I don't call the cops. You should be ashamed of yourself."

You're not alone in holding that opinion, but would you mind being a little more specific? "Look, I don't know what—"

Samantha's father raises his right forefinger; is standing on my parents' front lawn less than five feet away from me. His face is very white and his nose very red and his eyes an unfortunate coupling of both. "Save it, buddy. I'm a lawyer. I know how the legal system works, all right? Supplying drugs to an eighteen year-old girl is not something that the criminal system looks kindly upon, believe me, even if it is just pot."

Now it's my turn to instruct and enlighten with my finger. "You don't know what you're talking about," I say, pointing right back. "Your daughter, she's..." He's dropped his hand now and is listening, I can tell. "Your daughter, Samantha..."

"I know very well who my daughter is. My daughter Samantha what?"

"She's a good kid," I say.

Samantha's father peers at me like he's inspecting a bowl of soup for a hair. Satisfied it's particle-free, "Then stay away from her. It's hard enough for kids these days to do the right thing without having a frigging drug dealer living across the street."

"I'm not..." I sputter, before I can stop myself.

"You're not what? Don't lie to me. We both know what you are."

I pick my gloves up off the porch and slide them back on. "I'm not going to be around here much longer," I say, pointing at the For Sale planted in the middle of the yard.

"Good," he says.

"Yeah," I say.

And because that, apparently, is that, Samantha's father goes back the way he came and I go back inside the house. Where Buttercup Village's very own, home-grown dope dealer pours himself a big glass of red wine. I should be insulted, upset—irked, at least—but I'm not. That guy, he may not be much, he may be exactly who he seems like, but that guy, he's Samantha's father.

*   *   *

THEY HAVE STARBUCKS ON MOUNTAIN tops in Tibet, but not in Chatham. Theoretically, this is a good thing—anti-multi-national mumble mumble, locally-owned business et cetera. Practically, this only means that corporate head office definitely knows what it's doing, a four dollar cup of coffee as suspect to most Chathamites as paying for a book when you can get it for free from the library, or some pinko kook who doesn't support our troops (whatever it is they're doing over there, wherever *there* is). This also means that I'm waiting for Rachel at Coffee Time, the Tim Hortons down the street simply not appropriate for the sort of mid-afternoon *tête-à-tête* I have in mind. Location, location, location, even when you're just gently but firmly letting someone know it's not them, it's you.

The door opens, and the manufactured smile Rachel grants me upon entering doesn't make sense—I'm the one who's here to let someone down easy. If anyone is going to spare a stoical smile, it's me. Except she's also first off the mark with what I was going to lead with, tells me she's really glad we've had a chance to spend some time together since I've been back.

"Me too," I say which is easy to say, because it's true.

"But," Rachel says—but I was going to say *But*—"to be completely honest, I'm at a point in my life when I don't have time to spend on something that I know isn't going to work."

"Okay."

"Don't get me wrong," she says, placing her hand on top of mine. "You're a great guy. I know that sounds like some kind of kiss-off line, but it's true. Besides, you'll be going back to Toronto soon enough, and we're both too old for a long distance relationship."

True, true, and true. This time Rachel smiles a real smile, a smile borne of obvious relief, and it's a sunny Saturday afternoon and sometimes parting is such sweet, sweet ease and aren't we both so wonderfully civilized? In the Coffee Time parking lot the Chatham Classic Car Club is having their weekly whatever-you-call-it, men with their jackets undone standing around their vintage cars talking to other men standing around their vintage cars, the occasional hood lifted up to better appreciate the gleaming bad boy underneath. I know I should just be thankful things turned out the way they did, as easily as they did, but we've both still got coffee left in our cups, so what the hell, I ask what can't help but be on my mind.

"Just out of curiosity, what did you mean when you said you knew it wasn't going to work?"

Rachel squeezes my hand; you'd think we were on our second date, as opposed to just breaking up. "C'mon, Sam, let's just enjoy our coffee and this beautiful day. They say it might go up to as high as eleven by Monday. Can you believe it? It's about time. I'm so sick of winter." One day during grade eight math class we were told to put away our textbooks and forget everything we knew about what things weighed and how long things were and what the temperature was. Rachel must have been better at math than I was, I'm still a Fahrenheit and pounds and inches man.

"I'm not going to get upset," I say. "Like I said, I'm just curious."

"Sam, let it go, okay? I already said you're a great guy, and I meant it. Just take the compliment, all right?"

"All right." I sip from my coffee; Rachel does the same.

"It's just that you're the first woman I've been with since my wife, and I guess I want to make sure that whatever I did wrong I won't do again." Which isn't true, but which certainly sounds like it.

"Who said you did anything wrong?"

"No one. But you did say you knew it wasn't going to work, so I can only assume..."

Rachel puts down her coffee cup and stares out the window at the men buffing their cars and inspecting each other's motors, and then at me. "Like I said, it's nothing wrong with you, *per se*, it's just that who you are isn't—for me, understand, I'm just talking about myself—someone I can see myself with long-term. Okay?" She flashes a hopeful little smile.

"Okay. But you still haven't answered my question. What is it about me specifically that makes me a less than ideal long-term partner?"

"Geez, Sam..."

"C'mon, I can take it, I'm a big boy."

Rachel steels herself with the rest of her coffee. Setting down her cup, "You're selfish," she says.

"Okay." I promised to be a big boy, and big boys sit quietly until the person they're speaking to is finished speaking.

"Maybe selfish isn't the right word. But as far as I could tell, pretty much all you ever did when we weren't together, when you weren't visiting your dad, was write."

"How does that make me selfish? I'm a writer."

"Look, I'm not going to argue with you, Sam. I told you I didn't want to talk about this. You're the one who insisted."

"Okay, okay, but...it isn't odd to complain that a writer writes? That's kind of what they do."

"I wasn't complaining."

"Okay, but..."

This time when Rachel looks out the window I can tell she's attempting to figure out the best way to say what she's thinking.

"Maybe it's just because I've never known any other writers. Maybe it's an occupational hazard or something. But I got the feeling whenever we were together that even though you were there, you weren't really there, you know?"

"Not really, no."

Rachel looks out the window again. "It was as if doing things—life things, the kind of things that people do every day—wasn't very interesting to you. I got the feeling—and again, this could just be me—that you would have rather been off writing about something than actually doing it."

She's obviously tried hard to answer my question, so I give what she's said a moment to sink in.

"Well?" she says, stretching her mouth sideways into an exaggerated, hope-I-haven't-offended-you grin.

"I hear you," I say.

"But?"

"But honestly, I can't help but take what you're saying as a compliment."

"A compliment."

"Yeah."

Rachel exhales through her nostrils and stares at the ceiling. "It's not just about not wanting to do things, it's..." She turns her gaze on me. "It's like how you never asked me about my weight loss."

"I didn't think it was any of my business. And I didn't think it was the kind of thing you'd want to talk about."

"You're right. It isn't. And I wouldn't want to. But you should have asked me anyway. It would have shown you cared. About me. Or were at least interested in me. Interested in who I was."

"By asking you about something you wouldn't have wanted to talk about."

"That's right."

"I think I just figured out why things didn't work out between us," I say.

"Why's that?"

"Not because I'm selfish. Because I'm stupid."

Rachel laughs. Stands up and pulls on her coat. "Sam, I really am glad we got to hook up like we did. It's been an education."

I follow her lead and put on my jacket too. "Coming from a teacher, that can't be a bad thing."

Rachel is going to drive home, I'm going to walk—it really is a beautiful day—and we've hugged and promised to not let twenty-five years go by before the next time we talk. She gets into her car.

"And good luck with keeping CCI open," I say through the open window. "For what that's worth."

Rachel turns her key and the BMW roars to life. "Didn't I tell you?" she says. "We found out yesterday we lost. For good. It's closing for sure after this school year is done."

"I'm sorry," I say. "I know how much work you put into it."

Rachel shrugs, slips on her black Ray-Bans. "To tell you the truth, I'm actually sort of relieved. All the time I spent at meetings and getting petitions signed and all the rest of it, I'm excited to move on to what's next."

"And what's that?" I say. "What's next for Rachel Turnbal?"

"I don't know. I guess that's why it's exciting."

*   *   *

WHEN I'M NOT AT THAMES VIEW or writing, I sit in the park, I stand on the porch, I look out my front window. The nurses work to get Dad's fever and blood pressure down, only to watch them rise right back up, and Samantha has become invisible, no coincidence there, I'm sure. It's almost April—how the hell did that happen?—and some days I can get away with going outside in just a sweater. Today is one of them. I'm taking a break from working on the last chapter of my book; take my Mountain Dew to the window and look for someone who I know isn't there.

Who is here is the fat man on his mini-bike celebrating the increasingly fine weather by puttering around in grey track pants and a flowing white T-shirt, the slabs of his seat-bisecting ass slopping over each side. Thank you, spring.

And of course his fat wife is filming every momentous instant of his motorized exploits with her camera. Except that now, even though she's got her back to me, I can tell she's not fat anymore. And when the bike putt-putts past her and she turns around in the street to admire her darling's daring departure, the ten pounds she'd shed over the winter are hanging in a sling around her neck, the kid fat-cheeked just like his or her dad, but in a good way, a healthy baby way.

I step out onto the porch. It's almost warm. I've been inside all day, otherwise I might have known.

CHAPTER THIRTEEN

THIS TIME THE VOICE ON the phone doesn't reassure me that there's nothing to be unduly concerned about, just says I should come to Thames View as soon as possible, that my father's condition had worsened during the night. The time display on my cell phone says 1:12 AM. No one ever heard their phone ring at 1:12 AM and wondered if it was good news.

I call Uncle Donny for a ride while I pull on my pants, but there's no answer, he and my parents the last people on planet earth not to have an answering machine or voice-mail. Thames View would have notified him as well, so he's probably slept through the phone call. Typical Uncle Donny. I call a cab and stand on the porch in the dark and wait.

The ride over gives me plenty of time to imagine what to expect, but an empty bed and a dim, nightlight-lit silent ward wasn't one of them. I jog to reception where a skinny kid with faux-nerdy black framed-glasses and an alabaster complexion and a patchy red beard is holding a Japanese comic book six inches from his face.

"My father's not there," I say even before I stop running. "He's not in his bed."

The boy places his book face down on the counter top. "You must be Mr. Samson," he says.

I always think of that same stupid joke: Mr. Samson's my father, you can call me Sam. "Yeah," I say.

"No worries," he says. "Just take the elevator to the fifth floor and follow the sign to the intensive care unit. Mr. Samson—your father Mr. Samson—was moved there about an hour ago."

The miniature simulated waterfall near the elevator reuses its own dirty water to glug away serenely while I wait. *No worries.* Get back to me in another twenty years, Poindexter, then tell me *No worries.*

Thames View has its own topside state-of-the-art care facilities as well as private and semi-private rooms, but I don't need to ask the nurse at reception which room Dad is in, simply follow the sound of Frank Sinatra's voice. Uncle Donny must have had his ringer off when I called; he must have been here with Dad all along.

I don't say anything upon entering, just nod at the doctor and the nurse on either side of Dad's bed. The nurse is adjusting the line running from his left arm to the drip stand. The doctor is looking down at him like a parent watching a sick child sleep. Uncle Donny gets up from the chair by the window. The blinds are drawn and his boom box is perched on the window sill. When he doesn't speak, just comes and stands beside me, I know what I need to know.

The doctor fills in the details: probably a stroke in his sleep (without an MRI, Dad's essentially comatose condition makes an exact diagnosis difficult), likely sometime around midnight, system rapidly shutting down, heavily medicated and not in any pain; probably today or tomorrow at the latest.

"What's with the music, then?" I say.

The doctor's eyes meet Uncle Donny's; the doctor returns his attention to my father, says something to the nurse about the line.

"I don't care," Uncle Donny says. "He always loved these guys and he should be able to listen to them and enjoy them even if he can't tell us in so many words that that's what he wants. And I turned it down low like I was asked to—it's not going to bother anybody."

To the doctor, "It can't hurt, right?" I say.

The doctor puts his stethoscope to Dad's chest. "It can't hurt."

The doctor and the nurse come and go, Uncle Donny and I stay where we are. We listen to the Rat Pack live from the Sands in Las Vegas and watch Dad breathe. In a way, he looks better—calmer—than before the stroke. But, then, autumn leaves look most alive just before they fall. This isn't a metaphor, this is just the way that leaves are.

John F. Kennedy is in the Sands audience, and Sinatra introduces him from the stage. "What did you say his name was?" Dean Martin says. After Sammy Davis comes out to join them, Dean picks him up and holds him out to Frank. "Here," he says. "This award just came for you from the National Association for the Advancement of Coloured People."

Dad didn't like, Dad didn't dislike the Rat Pack—he listened to them because Uncle Donny liked listening to them. Uncle Donny wouldn't know what you were talking about if you tried to explain this to him, but I think he knows it. I think he knows it right now.

Uncle Donny stays with Dad while I go to get coffee from the machine in the lounge. I was never afraid of doctor's offices or hospitals, just don't like them because it's all so boring: the endless waiting, the cranky secretary's suspicion that you're wasting everyone's time, the doctors only guessing, after all, what's really wrong. Sara was the one who always made me go and see someone when I'd usually be quite content just to complain. She was the one who, if we were walking Barney at night and she thought she detected blood or worse in his crap, would bag it and carry it to the first streetlight and not care who noticed while she carefully checked.

When I get back to the room, Uncle Donny is sitting on the side of the bed, both hands holding one of Dad's. I put the coffee down on the side table.

"He was just like he was," Uncle Donny says. "Then he opened his mouth and made this sound like he was choking or something, then he stopped before I could get the nurse."

I sit down on the other side of the bed. In the movies, you know it's over when someone gently closes the patient's eyes, but Dad's eyes are already shut. Uncle Donny lets go of Dad's hand and gets up and turns off the CD, is giving me my moment alone with him, I know.

For a long time I thought Dad was already gone, thought I was already used to him being gone. I thought wrong. I don't know what I'm supposed to do, to say. "What's the date?"

"The date today, you mean?" Uncle Donny says.

"Yeah. What is it?"

"The second. No, wait. Today is tomorrow now. It's the third."

"Then my dad died the morning of April third."

Uncle Donny unplugs his boom box from the outlet, stands up and pulls the blind to the side. "It's still dark out," he says. "It's not morning yet."

"Then he died tonight, I guess."

"I guess."

*   *   *

UNCLE DONNY WANTED TO DRIVE me home after we were finished at Thames View, but I insisted on walking.

"It'll take you forty-five minutes to get there," he said.

"Who said I was going home?"

"Where the hell else would you go?"

"I'll talk to you this afternoon," I said.

I want to walk because I don't want to think, and I don't—not about Dad lying dead back at the hospital anyway, nor about him lying alive but dead in his bed at Thames View for the last how many months—but along the way to nowhere in particular I pass by an orthopedic footwear store that used to be where Lewis' Variety was, where my dad bought me a paperback copy of Jim Morrison's biography after I'd had my wisdom teeth removed because he knew I liked the Doors and in which I discovered that you could still be cool and get girls without being a jock. I walk by the St. Clair Grill where he and Mum and I used to go for Friday night dinner sometimes, the first restaurant where I was allowed to order for myself and the first nice restaurant I ever went to, the kind where you ate your cheeseburger deluxe with real silverware and the waitress kept coming back to make sure your water glass was full. I cross the street and pass the boarded-up building that was once the Aberdeen Tavern, where one Friday night in high school Steady Eddie and a bunch of us were coming out the door just as my dad and some guys from work were going in and all he said to me was to make sure that whoever was driving was sober and then he slipped me ten bucks. I cut down Emma Street, the street that was just a dirt road when Mum lived there as a teenager, and remember Dad saying how when they were first dating and he didn't have a car he'd walk from his house on Park Street to her house and back and that the round trip would take him two and a half hours, and when I asked him why he did it, he said because he'd wanted to see her. I shouldn't be, I know, but I'm smiling. Then I'm crying. Then I stop crying and am smiling again, and this time it's okay.

I don't know what time it is, I don't wear a watch—I've never understood why anyone would willingly wear that kind of urgent existential update on their arm—but Clem's Collectibles opens at 9:30 AM and the C'MON IN WE'RE OPEN sign has been flipped over and CFCO is playing today's contemporary country hits, although mercifully muted. It's been twenty-five years since I've been in here, a high-school wannabe boho looking for the sort of records that didn't get played on the radio and the kind of books that my teachers either weren't eager to tell us about or had never even heard of.

Although there are more porcelain cats and framed pictures of forgotten family members and 7UP bottles impersonating as antiques than anything potentially life-changing, there are also several red milk crates of old record albums, albeit now outnumbered two to one by used CDs and even a few battered cassette tapes. I flip, not expecting to find anything, and I don't, only the usual collection of junk store vinyl casualties: the Herb Alpert album with the woman on the front covered in whipped cream; one-time ubiquitous Leo Sayer in his high-top sneakers and coloured suspenders hurtling through the air to the top of the charts; the Liona Boyd LP with her in a flowing sheer dress and a guitar hanging across her back and sitting

210

atop a white horse in a meadow. All of them with the vinyl scratched, the cardboard covers scuffed, and their owners long ago having forgotten them.

"Are the books still in the back room?" I say to the woman behind the counter.

"Sure are."

Just for the hell of it, "Is Clem still around?" I say.

"Clem Sr. you mean?"

"Maybe."

"I'm Clem's granddaughter. Grandpa passed away a couple years ago. Can I help you with anything?"

"No, I'm"—I point to the rear of the store—"just going to take a look at the books."

Clem's granddaughter smiles, nods. "Happy huntin'," she says.

Past the cardboard boxes of obsolete printers and three-legged card tables and chipped tea cups and saucers are the books. The books, and Samantha browsing through them. She looks up from the paperback in her hands.

"I don't think I've ever seen anyone else back here," she says.

"I used to think the same thing."

"You used to come here too?"

"You think you're the only precocious teenager Chatham's ever had?"

"I'm not precocious," she says, sticking the book back on the shelf. "Just bored."

I look at the books and Samantha looks at the books, look at an entire wall of what Clem long ago decreed as CLASSICS to help differentiate these from, for instance, NOVELS (both bodice-rippers and the espionage variety), RELIGIOUS BOOKS (Bibles and inspirational how-to-go-to-heaven guides), HEALTH (*The Atkins Diet* books and *The*

New Atkins Diet books), and CELEBS (Shirley MacLaine spiritual tomes and Elvis Presley tell-alls). A "classic" according to Clem was anything that someone would have to read, like in school, as opposed to actually want to read.

"Have you ever read this?" I say, holding up a not-too tattered Grove paperback edition of *City of Night*.

"Nope."

"You should. You should get it. It's about a male prostitute trying to survive on the streets of L.A. in the '60s."

"This was obviously an influential book for you. Inspirational even?"

"It's well-written," I say. "That's inspiring enough."

I put *City of Night* back on the shelf and keep looking. It seems very important that I find Samantha a book.

"*Mrs. Dalloway*," I say, pulling it from the shelf. "A day in the life of one human being. Every thought and feeling and sensory impression."

"I've got enough to handle with every thought and feeling and sensory impression of my own."

"That's one of the reasons you read. To shake off the burden of selfhood, to realize that it's been the same shit, different century, for as long as we've all been here."

At least she bothers to take this one from me, even scans the back of the book. Handing it back, "I have a hard time getting into novels," she says. "I'm always thinking it can't be too important if it's just something that somebody made up."

I'm not sure if she's actively attempting to goad me or is just indifferent, but instead of offering further sagacious reflections upon the utility of literary prose, I stick the novel back into place.

"Looks like somebody else knows what I mean," she says, pulling a hardcover from one of the bottom shelves. She stands up and hands me the book.

It's one of my own novels, abandoned and apparently unread, the book mark stuck on page twenty-three. "No accounting for taste, I suppose," I say. The receipt is still inside. At least whoever got rid of it paid for it first.

"Or lack thereof."

Intentional or not, I take this as a peace offering. Shoehorning my novel back into place, "Why are you here and not in school?" I say.

"Why are you here and not at home working on your book?"

"My book's done," I say, which has nothing to do with how I came to be at Clem's Collectibles this morning, but which is also nothing that Samantha needs to know about. If you can't spread a little happiness, at least try not to increase its opposite.

"Congratulations," Samantha says.

"It's just a first draft."

"But still. It's sort of a big deal, isn't it?"

I liked to surprise Sara when I'd finish the first draft of a new book—tell her, "I'm done," and have her say, "Okay," thinking it was just that night's work that was finished, then I'd say, "No—I'm *done*." No matter what else she was doing, she'd drop it and we'd open a bottle of something and sit on the couch and allow me to feel like what I'd just done actually mattered.

"It's a good start," I say.

"So I guess no one's going to die tonight then," she says.

"No," I say. "Anyone who was going to die, they're at peace now."

We both scan the shelves again.

"I've actually got some good news too," Samantha says.

"Oh, yeah? What's that?"

"I got accepted into McGill."

"McGill? McGill University?"

"I'm pretty sure that's what they call it. Don't act so surprised."

"It's not that," I say. "I just thought you were going to apply to U of T."

"No, you wanted me to apply to U of T. I wanted to get as far away from my stupid family as possible and still go to a good school."

"I didn't know you were so … "

"Motivated? Together?"

"No, I … " Samantha laughs, which allows me to laugh; we laugh.

"So go ahead," she says. "Diss Montreal because it's not Toronto."

"Montreal is great," I say. "I bet you'll have a great time there. The main difference between the two cities isn't the language, it's that in Toronto people tend to have good taste in music but sit around listening to it in ugly buildings, whereas in Montreal there's all this beautiful architecture full of people listening to crappy music. It's a geographical and aesthetic conundrum for the ages."

"I think I can handle that."

"I'm sure you can."

I feel very hungry all of a sudden, which makes sense, and I don't need a book and Samantha doesn't need any of my recommendations. She can find her own books just fine.

"I'm hungry," I say.

"Okay."

"Where can I make that stop?"

"The mall?"

"God."

"You asked, I told. Don't shoot the messenger."

"Anyway, let's get out of here," I say. "This place smells mouldy."

"That's because it is mouldy."

Outside, it's definitely not mouldy; one hundred percent opposite, in fact, late-morning warmish windy and sunshiny and overall springtime springy. I shrug off my jacket and slip it over my shoulder. Samantha is wearing her usual black jeans, Converse, and hoody with the arms rolled down, but with the zipper undone at least. We stop at the corner; CCI is that way, the mall is this way.

"I guess I better get back," she says.

"C'mon," I say, "I'll buy you some poutine. It's the official carbo-load of your soon-to-be homeland."

"I was on a spare. I shouldn't skip too much anymore. My acceptance was conditional on me not flunking out."

"I don't think there's much danger of that," I say. "Besides, we've both got something to celebrate, right? It's not a good idea to let the good things in life go unobserved."

"Because it's bad karma or something?"

"No. Because they're so fucking rare."

And so we walk. And talk, about nothing in particular, just enough to justify ambling along side-by-side in such very pleasant weather toward what someone decades ago dubbed the Downtown Chatham Centre but no one has ever called anything but The Mall. Water finds its level, and people and places become what they are, even small-town shopping centers.

"I was just trying to help, you know," I say, the sunshine fooling me into speaking what's been on my mind for days now. "I didn't mean for you to feel bad."

"So we're talking about *that* now, are we?"

"I understand, it's none of my business."

215

"That's right, it isn't."

"I know."

Samantha stops walking. "You know, giving a shit isn't the worst thing in the world. I can at least … appreciate that. It was you thinking you could save me or something."

"I never thought that."

Samantha stares into traffic; stares long enough, I have time to realize I don't believe myself.

"You're right," I say.

She looks at me. "It's been recently brought to my attention," I say, "that maybe what's ordinary behaviour to me might be perceived by others as selfishness."

"Sounds like something somebody says when they're breaking up with somebody."

"Something like that. Anyway, maybe I wanted to help you not just because I wanted to help you, but because it helped me too."

"Helped *you*? How?"

"Write my book. My music book."

"You mean, like, writers' block or something?"

"More like the opposite." I look to lose myself in the sidewalk traffic, but there's barely a pedestrian trickle. "Thinking I was helping you helped me help myself. Helped me get something done that part of me didn't want to get finished."

Samantha starts walking again; so do I. "Did it work?" she says.

"I think so, yeah."

"You're not sure?"

"Who is?"

I open the door to the mall and we step inside and head for the escalator and the food court on the second level. There, just as we're walking by Sears, I grab Samantha's hand and pull her inside. Her flesh meshed into my mine is as surprising to me as it must be to her, but I don't want to argue about it, this is something we have to do.

"C'mon," I say.

"C'mon where?"

"You'll see."

Some things—most things—change, but Sears isn't one of them. Not too much, anyway. The houseware section is still stocked with bedside lamps and massaging chairs and sock organizers and clocks. Lots and lots of clocks. There isn't the wind-up kind anymore, but there are floor model wall clocks and bedside clock radios, some with built-in iPod docks and some without, and even a few cheaply made grandfather clocks. I let go of Samantha's hand and lay out the plan like a veteran quarterback in the huddle.

"Just pretend like you're looking around, like everything you see is a delight to the eye. And every clock you see that has any sort of alarm, set it for two minutes, then four minutes, then six minutes, then eight minutes past one. I'll be doing the same, but with the odd numbered minutes. Don't let on that we know each other. Just act like you're giving each clock a careful once over before you make your purchase. When you're done, meet me over by the linen section, right over there."

"Can I ask why?"

"No," I say. "Now go."

She rolls her eyes, she stands there doing nothing while I get busy, she eventually, reluctantly, languidly, sets to work: pushing buttons, clicking switches, finally finishing and moving on to her next ticking task.

Five minutes later, we've rendezvoused by the duvets. "Now what do we do?" she says.

"Now we wait and watch."

The grandfather clock loudly chimes its time, and the salesman in his sports jacket and Sears badge raises an eyebrow, but calmly walks over to silence it.

"And?" Samantha says.

"And keep watching."

Which we both do—watch the same man step behind the cash register to check out a customer only to have to excuse himself to quiet a shrieking clock radio, only to return to his register and have another clock radio beep beep beep and then another and then another keep him bouncing back and forth between the floor and the till as the lineup at the cash register grows longer and the people in it smile wider.

"Well?" I say

Samantha is smiling too, although not as much as I thought she would. "You've done this before, I take it?"

"My friend Eddie and I used to do this all the time when we were in high school."

"*All* the time?"

"Okay. Once in awhile. Anyway, it's a classic. It'll never grow old."

"Except pretty soon everyone will set the alarm on their phones and there won't be any such thing as clock radios anymore."

The man behind the cash register is shaking his head and apologizing to the woman whose flat screen TV he's scanning.

"Let's go and eat," I say. "I don't think I've ever been hungrier in my life."

CHAPTER FOURTEEN

I WAS AGAINST HAVING A FUNERAL ceremony because there was only Uncle Donny and me, but he convinced me that it wasn't true, that there were other people who would want to say goodbye.

"Like who?" I said.

"Some of the guys he worked with," he said. "Some of the guys we grew up with."

"Then why didn't any of them come and see him when he was at Thames View?"

"Some of them did. At the beginning. But after awhile, you know, I mean ... "

I did know. After awhile, there wasn't much point in visiting someone who isn't them anymore and who doesn't recognize who you are either. That's what family is for.

Uncle Donny was right; it was the right thing to do. I didn't know most of the people there, and the ones that I did know I didn't know well, but it was good for them to see Dad one last time and it was good for Uncle Donny and me to be reminded that before he was what he became, he was him. We watched them put the casket with Dad in it into the earth next to my mother.

* * *

THE PEOPLE WHO WANTED TO BUY the house were still interested when I asked Laura to contact them, and all we had to do was knock two thousand dollars off their counter-offer to get the deal done. What the hell. I'm glad for the money—glad to be free of my mounting Visa bill most of all—but I'm also glad that somebody who actually likes the house will get to live in it. Everything I'm keeping is packed into three boxes, and I've left the beds and the practically brand new fridge and stove and the dresser drawers and all the rest of it for the buyers. A young couple can always use a jump start on their new life.

The windows are open—the windy but almost-warm day deserves it—and while I'm double-checking room-by-room that I haven't forgotten anything, I see Samantha not sitting, but actually swinging on the swing. It's a little after one o'clock on a Saturday afternoon and the park isn't ours alone, there's a small boy and his father attempting to fly a kite.

"Hey," I call though the bedroom-window screen.

"Spring cleaning?" she says.

"More or less. Come on over."

Samantha goes up, comes back down—"All right," she says—goes up, comes back down.

In the time it takes her to knock on the front door, I've finished making my rounds, anything that I've left behind destined to go missing forever. It was a good thing I was so careful: at the back of my dad's empty underwear drawer, several unopened Lifesavers Books, the gift I gave him every year at Christmas as soon as I started making lawn-cutting money because he let me believe he liked them so much.

"Still knocking when you don't have to," I say, letting her in.

"There are worse habits than politeness."

Once we're standing in the living room surrounded by all of my stuff—the boxes, my suitcase, my laptop, the record albums I've eBay-accumulated since I've been in Chatham—it's clear that there isn't much left to say. Which is fine, but isn't the greatest timing. Life rarely breaks down into a tidy three-act structure. Too bad for life. Too bad that it's too bad.

"What time's your train?" Samantha says.

"My Uncle's picking me up around 2:30."

We both survey the room, searching for something to see. I see something first.

"Why don't you take this?" I say, going over to the record player and receiver and speakers still plugged in, but almost forgotten on the floor by the couch.

"I don't have any records."

"You could get some. Even the cooler whipper-snapper bands that you're into are doing vinyl pressings these days. And you know by now how much better they sound than what you hear on an iPod."

"So you say."

"Because it's true." I unplug the cord and put the speakers on top of the turntable's dust cover.

"But what am I going to do with it when I go to Montreal?" she says.

"Take it with you. Why wouldn't you take it with you? Just promise me you'll get a new needle sooner than later. You owe it to your records."

Samantha smiles, shrugs, puts out her hands for me to load her down. Which I do, but there's one more thing she needs.

"Pick one," I say, fanning the records across the kitchen table.

"Those are the ones you paid a lot for on eBay, though, aren't they?"

"Not so much. Anyway, I can afford it. Set the record player down for a minute and choose one. You need a record if you're going to have a record player. And this way at least I'll know you got a good one to start with."

In spite of herself, once she starts going through the pile I can see she's becoming interested. She takes in the covers; she scans the back of the albums; the ones that are gatefolds she can't help but open up and inspect. "I don't know any of these people," she says. "How would I know which ones I'd like?"

"They're all good, believe me."

"That doesn't mean I'd like them all."

"Just go with your gut, then," I say. "Pick one that jumps out at you."

She works through the pile again backwards, stops at Mother Earth's *Bring Me Home*.

"Who's this?" she says.

"Tracy Nelson is the lead singer. She's the real deal. Sort of R&B, sort of folk-rocky, kind of hippie-country. What made you choose this one?"

Samantha holds up the record. "I liked the picture of the dog on the back."

It's then that I recognize that it's a sealed record, that that was the reason I'd bought it online. Samantha can tell I'm not thinking about the photo of Tracy Nelson's dog.

"If you want to keep it, that's cool," she says, placing it on top of the pile.

"It's not that," I say. "It's just that it's a sealed record."

"Does that make it more valuable or something?"

"Yeah, but that's not what's so great about a sealed record."

"What is?"

"For one thing, they've never been played, so they'll never sound better than the first time you place the needle on the opening track. If they're original pressings like this one, they're also a time capsule. This particular record came out in 1971, and it's literally still 1971 inside that cellophane wrapper. And best of all, if you've never heard the actual music somewhere else before, you can't be disappointed, your entire life might change with one single song, there's no way of knowing it's not going to happen as long as that wrapper is still on. A sealed record is about as close to perfection as you can get."

"But if you don't open them, they're pretty much useless, right?"

"I suppose you could look at it that way too."

We both look at *Bring Me Home* by Mother Earth, Reprise Records, 1971.

"Is she—the lead singer—what's her name?"

"Tracy Nelson."

"Right—Tracy Nelson. Is she, you know, one of those people you might have written about?"

"One of the people who died, you mean?"

"Right."

"You tell me," I say.

"What do you mean? Is she or isn't she?"

"I've got a new book I want to start on once I get home. A novel this time. Tracy Nelson belongs to you now. And don't use your fingernail to open the seal. Use something sharp, like a steak knife. What you want is a nice clean opening all the way across. But leave the rest of the wrapper on. It's not the same as having a sealed record, but it's the next best thing."

ABOUT THE AUTHOR

IAN WILLMS

RAY ROBERTSON is the author of the novels *Home Movies*, *Heroes, Moody Food, Gently Down the Stream, What Happened Later*, and *David*, as well as the non-fiction collections *Mental Hygiene: Essays on Writers and Writing* and *Why Not? Fifteen Reasons to Live*. Born and raised in Southwestern Ontario, he lives in Toronto.